A Cast of Crabs

Edited by
Gaynor Jones

ISBN eBook: 978-1-9196087-9-2
ISBN print: 978-1-9196087-8-5

Retreat West Books
retreatwest.co.uk/books

Contents

Foreword

BOTH GAYNOR AND I are delighted to bring you the latest in our annual anthology series from the Retreat West Prize. This year we have 30 stories included as we added the new Micro Fiction category and we hope you enjoy these mini masterpieces as much as we do.

Our thanks go to our judges who chose the winning stories from the outstanding shortlists of ten stories they were sent. Kirsty Logan chose our winners in the Short Story Category: First Place – The Jellyfish at the Traffic Lights by Susan Iona Swan; Second Place – The Visitor by Emma Naismith; and Third Place – A Trip to the Island One Last Time by Catherine Ogston.

Our Flash Fiction judge was Michelle Elvy and she awarded First Prize to Button Bus by Chris Cottom; Second Prize – The Weathering by Martha Lane; and Third Prize – A Cast of Crabs by Bernadette Stott.

The Micro Fiction winners were chosen by Tim Craig: First Prize – Scratch Art for Grown-Ups by Sally Curtis; Second Prize – America by Sherri Turner; and Third Prize – Body of Christ by Moira Grath. Congratulations to all our top prize winners and all of the shortlisted authors.

When we started this annual prize back in 2015, I'd envisaged it running for many years, but everything changes and this is the penultimate book from Retreat West. We have one more anthology coming in 2023 from this year's prize, which is going to be the last one we run. Sadly, the costs of publishing mean we can no longer continue with the books, but we are excited about our new online journal, *West*Word, which launches with a special edition this autumn and opens for submissions in January 2023.

We hope you'll carry on reading with us as we take a new publishing direction.

Amanda Saint

The Jellyfish at the Traffic Lights
Susan Iona Swan

THE SIREN WOKE me last night. When four ascending notes followed, warbling in that eerie way they do, I knew today would be rough.

'Careful when you're wading,' Zach warned before he left for work. 'It's spring tides and the equinox. The water will be high.'

I dress the kids in waders and buoyancy aids and hustle them downstairs. The water is only halfway up the washboard. We don't need the canoe. The school is on slightly higher ground so the water level will lower as we approach.

It's a mess outside. A shell of a car has washed into our road, bladder wrack strewn across its roof. A cluster of mussels is attached to the bumper and I have a vision of Zach and me, a lifetime ago, eating *moules frites* at a café in Montmartre.

We're splashing through ankle deep water on the High Street when we see it: a mess of translucent rubbery flesh as big as a satellite dish. The frilly arms are as thick as mine and are tangled in the railings on the traffic light island. It must have got trapped when the tide went out. I'm weighed down by sadness. A bloom of jellyfish is a wonder to behold; they grace the sea like underwater ballerinas.

'Wow,' says Mia, 'That's a Portuguese Man o' War. Or, a Portuguese *Person* o' War as Grandma would say. They can kill you.'

'It's too big for that and the colours aren't pretty enough. It's a barrel jellyfish. Huge but harmless.'

Most things out there are harmless. Compared to us.

'Is it dead?' Sami asks.

'I'm not sure. They die after an hour out of water but this one's still semi-immersed.'

Three lads in school uniform run over and prod it with their bare feet. Flouting the law in one of the few ways they can these days – No Wading Without Waders – the signs are everywhere. A fishy smell reaches my nostrils and the kids wrinkle their noses.

'There's hundreds on the beach,' says one of the lads, 'Portuguese Mans o' War.'

Before Mia corrects him I say, 'They're barrel jellyfish.' One of the lads kicks it so the flesh wobbles. I flinch. 'Hey, don't do that.'

'What you are? Jellyfish police?'

'She's a marine biologist,' Sami pipes up.

I wish. Excitement stirs when I remember the tip-off

from my mate Keira who works at the Environment Agency: the new jobs are being advertised today.

'Liar. She works in the supermarket. I've seen her.'

'But in the marine section,' I say, deadpan. It's not far from the truth. They had me rearranging the shelves for Water Wear yesterday – new season wet suits and rubber boots in neon colours.

One of the lads peers at me. 'Is it still alive?'

'Hard to tell. They don't have lungs or hearts, or brains come to that.'

'Brainless,' the lads echo, laughing. I feel offended for some reason.

'Can we go by the beach, Mum? See the jellyfishes?' Sami asks. I check my phone. We probably have time but I loathe going to the beach. It stirs memories of when I was young and we'd play on the acres of golden sand and lie in the lapping waves. Now it's a raging mass of angry water.

I lift the kids onto the high wall of the sea defence so they can see. Even though the tide is out, no sand is visible. Danger No Swimming, read the signs. Beyond the wall is what used to be a park and a coastal road. The broken chunks of concrete are a graveyard to a swarm of decaying flesh. They used to wash up in summer but now they are swept in all year round. In two hours' time the tide will be high enough to wash them over the wall and by noon they'll be slapping the glass front of the supermarket.

My scientific brain kicks in. Jellyfish feed on the zoo-plankton released by algae blooms that grow near the shore. The blooms are increasing in the over-warm, acidic seas. What if jellyfish can't cope with this over-abundance? Or is it something in the algae that's affecting them? If they die then so will the turtles that feed on them. And just like that the eco balance tips and falls. And another thing bothers me, the fact we're eating them; jellyfish are the main ingredient in this weird pink thing we sell in Frozen – lobster roll. It doesn't say 'jellyfish' on the pack, of course, it says 'scyphozoa', but they can't fool me, the marine biologist who isn't a marine biologist.

A recycling vehicle whirs along and operatives scrape them up with spades. My eyes slip beyond to the slate grey sky and churning sea, to the peaks of the waves whipped and foamed by the wind. How amazing that for millennia, the sea knew where to stop and when to retreat. It had a daily, monthly, annual behaviour so predictable that we organised our fishing and tourist industries around it. We farmed it, mined it and har-nessed it for energy but we never cared for it. Now it's like a neglected elderly relative – volatile and demented.

I don't chat at the school gates; my shift starts in fifteen minutes. The information board says, high tide 15.00, pick up 18.00. Could be worse. 'It's almost a normal day,' I say to the kids, handing them their shoes and kissing them goodbye. Don't say 'normal' in front of them, Zach would say, to them this fuckedupness is normal. 'You can have a nice play later. I'll come and pick you up in the canoe.' Thank God the school has the go-ahead for a rooftop playground so one day they can spend some time in the fresh air.

The water is only halfway up my shins but the waders keep my jeans dry. Along the High Street, shopkeepers are removing washboards and sweeping out. On the super-market window I read today's opening hours: 9–12.00. It will be 14.00 before they let me go, only one hour off high water. I clamber over the sandbags and splash across the ground floor to the backyard, wincing at the genera-tor's roar.

'I need this lot on fruit and veg toot sweet,' the man-ager says waving at some crates. I stare at the green apples, purple plums, yellow pears and red strawberries. It should make me feel better, that there are places where trees still blossom, crops flourish and vegetables grow in peaty earth but all I feel is envy for those who live on higher ground: those people living normal lives in normal times who don't have to plan their days around the six hours of low water and deal with their homes flooding twice a day.

After heaving boxes of potatoes onto the trolley, I push it to the lift. I signal to the manager I'm going up in case it dies like last week and no one notices. Luckily, I was stocking the biscuit aisle and had a ready supply of custard creams; I can't see potatoes offering the same comfort. When the loud speaker announces 'till operators to stations', I swap my waders for shoes and I'm at mine by the time the crowd funnels upstairs. I groan quietly as in a matter of minutes, twenty customers line up with baskets. My conveyor belt isn't working and after hauling their shopping from one side to the other, I wait while they scrabble inside their bags for money. Why does payment always come as a surprise?

***

I WADE HOME with my shopping bag on my head. At the front door, water laps the top of the washboard. I can't resist a peek at our living room. The floor is black with slime and the smell of rotting vegetation makes me retch. Sea lettuce is draped over the windowsills. On the mantelpiece, a mermaid's purse has been left. Imagine; shark's eggs where there used to be flames. I raise my eyes to the ornate cornice and ceiling rose, the only testament to how pretty our Victorian terrace house once was.

We always wanted to live by the sea, and here we are, living in it.

At the top of the stairs I pull off my waders and tackle the triple mortice lock on the landing door. I don't have to pick up the kids until 17.30, so I have three hours of freedom. Stuck indoors, alone. No wonder Internet porn and sex toys are the major growth industries. But it's time to indulge in my own fantasy.

At least the power is on. I edge around the table and chairs, clear the kids' toys from the bed, and sink into the cushions with my laptop. I laugh when I type, 'Environment Agency', and my search engine predicts I want 'flood search'. Bit late for that. When Zach and I checked ten years ago, before we bought this house, it was in Flood Zone 1, the lowest risk. We wouldn't have got our crippling mortgage otherwise. They hadn't accounted for how fast the ice would melt towards the end, in the same way sand filters through an egg timer. Turns out, science isn't an exact science. We were in the realm of the unknown, great at collecting data and analysing the results but not so great at predicting what they meant: how high water levels would rise and how much land would be submerged. The guiding ethos of the Scientific Advisory Group for Emergencies seemed to be, *sic tantum bonum*, so far, so good. That bloody virus knocked climate change off the agenda. We didn't want more gloom and doom. It's odd to think that the only people who got it right were the novelists, and they, by their own admission, write fiction. The sound of a siren draws me to the window. An ambulance is careering up the road, its wake slapping the walls of the houses. Fiction is the new fact.

Where will we go when this house is condemned? We can't afford to move to higher ground and what's high today won't be so high in ten years' time. If only my parents had bought a larger plot we could have added another caravan. I haven't the heart to tell Zach it's pointless to build a houseboat, that we'll never get a river mooring. We're not key workers or vulnerable so we're way down the list.

But now we have a way out.

I click to 'Jobs' and there it is, just as Keira told me.

'Marine biologists required to monitor the environmental impact of floating cities.'

1. To log the loss of bio-diversity caused by sewage, grey waste and plastics disposal
2. To study the extent of disease in fish and seaweed farms
3. To monitor the incidence and consequences of overfishing and species extinction
4. To record how marine fuel emissions affect both human and sea life

It's my dream job. A chance to use my skills. I'd be working in a lab in Plymouth so I'd be forced to take virus tests every two days and I'll have a trek to higher ground to the bus stop each day but I'd be that golden thing – a government employee, entitled to a keyworker apartment in a floating city.

I follow the link to *New World*, the modestly named company who builds them. A digital mock-up shows around ten huge cruise ships connected with movable bridges. Fifty thousand people could live there. There are schools, health centres leisure facilities and supermarkets. Blimey. There's even a casino. Apartments start at 1.5 million. That's crazy. It's more expensive than an apartment on high ground in Tidal Zone 2. Crewmembers have rooms in the hold and that's where the affordable housing for key workers is located. Hmm. Would I want my family to live in the bowels of a ship? How would these floating cities fare in storms? I click back to the Environment Agency site. What I read chills me. The ships run on a high-sulphur marine fuel that would cause higher carbon emissions than in Greater London in 2030, before they banned petrol and diesel. Seriously? Is the only solution to living on our overheated planet to heat it further? I don't know whether to protest their construction or crawl into a hole.

The tidal app on my phone pings and I glance at the screen. Atlantic storm Ahmed is rolling in. Great. Wahid just left and now we're running through the alphabet again. A headline flashes: Jellyfish Wash up in Huge Numbers. I swear this phone can read my mind. It's happening all along the coast; not just here. I want to finish reading the article but I don't have time. While there's still power, I make quornfish cakes for tea and heat peas and chips in the microwave. Then I fill in the application form.

I'm manoeuvring the canoe downstairs when it strikes me that the council were clearing those jellyfish very promptly. Suddenly, I know what I have to do. I run back inside for a rope.

In the street the water is thigh-high but falling. I move carefully, judging the position of kerbs and bollards. When I round the corner the wind whips my hair. Storm Ahmed is blowing waves along the road.

The sight of the children holding hands and wading across the playground towards me makes me cry. I'm seized by an overwhelming sense of having let them down, that I should have done better. Love laced with pity and guilt. I'm worn out trying to give them security in an insecure world; of pretending the abnormal is normal. Do other parents think like this? I could never take that job even if I was offered it. Zach can't always do the school run; the hours are too erratic. The supermarket shifts mean I can fit work around the kids and we eat well. How could I think anything else was feasible?

I hug them and they climb into the canoe and each pick up a paddle even though I'm towing them.

The jellyfish is still at the traffic lights.

'Can we release it, Mum?' Mia asks.

I smile a secret smile. 'Better still, let's take it home. It can stay in the living room.'

'Yay,' they cry in unison.

Later, I'll call Keira and arrange a time to take it to the lab.

I bend down and curl my fingers around the squidgy, unearthly arms and feed them through the railings. It's as if it was trying to hold on, to resist washing out to sea again, to avoid drifting out of control. I tie the rope around one of its arms and we tow it home, trailing tentacles and broken limbs. I feel a profound sense of camaraderie. For what am I, if not a creature at the mercy of the tides?

The Visitor
Emma Naismith

WHEN BARBARA ANSWERED the door on a concrete
Monday morning, she found herself standing face to face
with what appeared to be a curly-haired salesman.
Shimmery-shined shoes glistened in the rain, droplets
rolled down his Macintosh and he wiped the drips from
his forehead to reveal a remarkably white-toothed smile.

'Don't sell me anything,' she began, one hand palm
out in front of her, one hand clutching her remote
control.

'Is Frankie at home?' This question threw her and she
looked over his shoulder thinking perhaps he was not a
salesman after all despite the teeth and the shoes and the
raised eyebrows. Sure enough there was no bag packed
with brushes or books or cleaning products.

'Oh God, does… did Frankie owe you money?' She
could feel her knuckles crackling under her grip. She let
go of the remote control so it dropped with a thud.

'No, no, it's not that,' he shook his head like a dog so
that tiny speckles of rain flew off him.

'Frankie was not religious. And neither am I,' she said. It must be about souls. Surely. He looked so pure, despite the rain and the grime and the traffic.

'I have a product for him.' He gave her the white-gleam smile again then reached for the opening flap of his shoulder bag and she heard the Velcro rip in a single slice of sound.

'Frankie doesn't have a penny. In fact, my friend, Frankie has less than a penny, he has less than a fraction of a quarter of a slice of penny and if he's been buying things from you then, I'm sorry but it all stops here. IT ALL STOPS HERE. FRANKIE IS DEAD.' Barbara regretted shouting the last bit almost immediately as it wasn't really meant for the doorstep seller, it was meant for Frankie. But Frankie was not in earshot.

BARBARA WAS MINDING her own business the second time he came to the door. She had been doing the crossword, with the television on in the background, across from the armchair still in the shape of Frankie. She'd nodded off, as so often happens when three bars are on the fire and the room has warmed up and the clue is rather difficult, when the knock came. He was just as shiny this time but more insistent. And she noticed his eyelashes glistened.

'It's Frankie's poem.' He held an envelope out to her.

'Oh Jesus Lord Above, save me! Frankie turned to

poetry in his last days, did he now,' Barbara told the ceiling.

'I might as well give it to you, as it's written. And now that Frankie's gone,' said the poet in the doorway.

'You wrote a poem for Frankie?' she asked.

'On behalf of him really. He didn't have the words,' he said. 'Well he had the words, but not the glue, if you know what I mean.'

'Did you even know Frankie?'

'Do we know anyone really?'

'Oh Lord, he did owe you money, didn't he?' Barbara asked, leaning forward, but caught a glimpse of the sky so she pulled back in.

'There is no obligation,' said the lad, who Barbara saw now was much younger than she first thought. The skin on his face was taught, hairless.

She closed the door.

The envelope came through the letterbox. Barbara posted it back out again.

THE THIRD TIME he came, he didn't say anything but stood in the doorway getting wet. Barbara wondered if the doorstep poet salesman could smell shoe polish. Frankie's shoes were still lined up straight as train tracks under the jackets on the pegs beside the door. Polished night after night. *A new start tomorrow*, he'd say, and then the work would call in the morning and she'd tell them, *not today*, and she'd close the bedroom door on Frankie.

So Barbara invited the poet in. If they were going to read poems then they wouldn't be doing it in the rain with the number 44 bus groaning behind them, sending up puddle-mud and grime. This would be done properly.

She wasn't really sure where to put the doorstep seller at first. As they stood in the hall while Barbara made up her mind whether to take him to the kitchen or the living room, she noticed his smell over the polish; a metallic, sweet scent. She decided the kitchen, as then she could keep an eye on him while the kettle boiled. There hadn't been anyone in the house since Frankie died, so she wasn't really used to it.

They drank tea and he handed her the envelope. 'For Frankie', it said on the front. Barbara noticed his broad shoulders.

'I don't think I can open it today.'

'I'll come back tomorrow.'

WHEN HE CAME back, he asked if she wanted to read it outside instead. So Barbara had to explain to him that she doesn't go outside. It's not really that strange you see. She is inside. Where she always is. So that the sky is not directly above her head. When it is, she told him, it reminds her of the turn of the earth and that plays havoc

15

with her sense of balance. It's nothing really, but the earth does seem to be turning more quickly now that Frankie's gone. Shame it doesn't make the days shorter.

So she invited him in but put the poem on the hall table. The salesman was good at the crossword. He sat in Frankie's chair and helped her with the clues although he didn't like thinking with the television on so he'd snatch the remote control and switch it off. Barbara pretended to be angry and sent him off to make more cups of tea as a punishment. He shimmered. And he'd do the shopping, which she had to admit was a real help, as the deliveries she'd been ordering were never quite right.

ONE DAY, WHEN he was leaving to go, she could smell the polish from Frankie's shoes and hear the rain pummelling outside.

'You'll catch your death out there.'

So she put him in the spare room. She doesn't call it the guest room as she never has guests. Before bed they'd drink more tea and look out the window. Barbara could look at the sky through glass. That way it didn't spin. And the salesman knows a whole lot about the stars. She made sure they didn't look out the windows at the side of the house, which overlook the garage. It's too easy to get pictures in your head before bedtime.

ONE NIGHT SHE walked in on him in the shower. Forgetting. So hard to remember you are alone and then all of a sudden so hard to remember there is someone there. And there, between his legs, nothing. A blankness. 'I'm so sorry.'

THE NEXT DAY he watered all the plants, made the tea and solved the last crossword puzzle. Barbara folded the newspaper away, patting it.

'We'll start a new one tomorrow. You've really got a knack with these.'

Later when he explained that there were many like him walking the earth, ones that had something to pay back, latched onto the sadness of somebody, until it disappears, earning their wings, again, she didn't understand.

'I was assigned Frankie,' he told her later, 'Not just the poem.'

'I don't understand a thing you are talking about. Is it money you're after?'

THE POEM SAT unopened on the hall table. Barbara passed it every night when she started the wheezy climb to bed. But it felt as if opening it would be ripping open her heart. So she left it until tomorrow, beside Frankie's shoes.

And on the landing upstairs peeked into the guest room at the visitor. She wished she could touch the blonde curls. And then on into her empty bed. Where Frankie retreated so much of the time. And all she wanted was for him to get up out of that bed and put in a hard day's work. And now all she wants is for him to be back in this bed. And how can you want both things so desperately when it is impossible. Impossible.

In the morning Barbara put on the television loud so she couldn't hear her thoughts or the visitor's answers to the crossword. She let the cup of tea he made grow cold on the worn arm of her armchair and put on all three bars of the heater even though she knows it stunts the growth of his wings. She understands now. He came for Frankie and stays for her.

But then he went out and she wished he hadn't and she made fish and chips and mushy peas for his dinner. Real chips, mind, fried twice and dripping fat into kitchen roll and smothered in vinegar and so much salt that they had to make pot after pot of tea and it made them laugh.

FRANKIE'S SHOES DISAPPEARED from the hall and Barbara didn't mind. She didn't miss the smell of polish and instead she put a table there and pot plants on it. She stood in the hall admiring them. And when the visitor passed the plants glowed.

They played scrabble and when it got dark he told her there was a meteor shower in the Pleiades star cluster that they should see. Barbara noticed Frankie's armchair was no longer Frankie's shape.

'It's no big deal if I watch it from the window, is it?' she asked.

'You'll see it better from outside,' he told her.

'Ach on you go and enjoy yourself.' She told him and watched the swellings from his shoulder blades as he went out the back door. They had certainly grown since he arrived.

BARBARA ASKED HIM about Frankie, about why he hadn't been able to shake off the sadness. She felt brave that day. He tried his best, he told her, with his smile.

THE VISITOR'S WINGS became full. Downy soft.

'We did a good job of those,' said Barbara. 'Who'd have thought they'd grow so big.'

'Saturn is visible tonight. Just below the moon.'

'I'll come outside and see it.'

THE VISITOR HELD the door open for a long time as Barbara bustled and shuffled around the sitting room. 'I'll be right there.'

On the threshold she stopped. The cold night air coming into the house. The visitor held out a hand, Barbara took it.

'Ooh you have lovely warm hands. Let's see this planet then.'

They walked through the door frame, down the steps and up the path to the centre of the grassy patch, which Barbara has not seen up close for months. Barbara looked up. The sky was blustery dark. Just the silhouette of wings against the purple grey. The sky didn't spin and she couldn't tell if the earth was moving. The visitor stood behind her pointing at Saturn. And she saw the moon and the planet and tiny prickles of stars then something, a bat or a moth, fluttered. A foggy crumpling above her. Ascending. And then she went back inside and opened the envelope.

A Trip to the Island, One Last Time
Catherine Ogston

'I FEEL TRAVEL sick,' announced a small voice from the passenger seat.

'How is that possible?' said Jenny. 'You don't have a stomach or eat food.'

There was no answer as the car wound its way around bends. The roads were quiet, the usual tourists posing in front of waterfalls and snowy hills nowhere to be seen.

'You're right,' said Cleo. 'I think what I am feeling is a manifestation of your anxiety and trepidation.'

Jenny considered arguing that she felt neither of those things but said nothing. The doll had an answer for everything and it was nothing like the advert had promised. 'Perfect companion' was what had been proffered; akin to a labrador but able to hold conversations and stave off lockdown loneliness.

'Can I send it back?' Jenny had asked the person on the other end of the helpline after three days of Cleo giving unwarranted advice and expressing disdain for her wallpaper choices and nightly white wine habit. The voice had told her *no, it was all in the small print, she had read the small print, hadn't she?*

'No!' said Jenny, then muffled her voice so as to not alert Cleo to the conversation. 'Nobody reads the small print! Can I at least turn it off?'

That was also a negative. There was no off switch and the doll had been fitted with a battery that would last three months. *Your Loneliness Buddy will adapt to your needs and intuitively become your perfect lockdown mate,* the voice had said before Jenny disconnected the call in frustration.

'Would you like to converse?' said Cleo. 'We could discuss current topical issues.'

'Christ, no,' said Jenny. 'I want to forget the news, thanks very much.'

She leaned over and pressed various buttons on the car radio but was only met with static. There was no signal after the first hour of driving. It stopped at Loch Earn, the reception dipping in and out until nothing at all.

'How much longer?' said Cleo and Jenny ignored her.

Everything about the route was familiar even though she hadn't driven it for nearly a year. There were the same white-washed hotels, the same patches of pine forest, the same strange tree growing out of a boulder as the car climbed the incline of the Glencoe landscape. She shouldn't be here. She suspected Cleo knew that too.

'How will we get in?' said Cleo.

'I know where the spare keys are,' said Jenny.

'What if he changed them?'

Getting a locksmith over from the mainland to change the locks didn't seem likely in the middle of pandemic. 'Hardly an essential journey,' said Jenny.

'Neither is this, is it?' Cleo said and Jenny considered unrolling the side window and throwing the small figure into a lochan of dark icy water.

Eventually they reached the road that hugged the coast line. The day was cloudy, making the sea grey and uninteresting. Jenny was glad; if the sun had been shining—picking out silver ridges of sparkling water, turning the west coast sky cornflower blue, bouncing brightly in the windows of chocolate-box cottages—it would have been too much.

Then they were turning off the main road and driving down the single track road to Kilconan. Usually this was when Jenny felt escalating excitement, bone-scouring relief that she was going to make the evening ferry; her reward for racing out of work and driving, rally-style, for near enough three hours. But today there was only acid in her stomach. She pulled over in a passing place, flung open her door and threw up on the verge.

Cleo managed to say nothing for at least a minute after Jenny had righted herself.

'The sensible option is to go back,' she said. 'Why are

we doing this anyway?'

Jenny shut the door and drove off again. 'It's a fact-finding expedition.'

The road narrowed as they reached its end and they pulled up to an unusual amount of spaces on the grassy roadside; empty gaps left by city-stuck people.

Jenny parked, tucked one mirror in and locked the car. She took a few steps and then went back and double-checked the lock. 'Habit,' she muttered to Cleo as she stuffed the doll into her rucksack and threatened it with being quiet.

The walk down the stone pier made Jenny's legs shake. It was a rush of memories and feelings and the interminable sensation that it shouldn't be like this. She should be looking at the small blue and white foot-ferry, bobbing gently in the water, and have excited joy flooding her synapses. Instead there was only hurt and unanswered questions.

'Still time to be reasonable and get back in the car,' said a voice, stern and teacherly, from inside the bag.

But at that moment the ferrymen appeared in their oilskins and heavy boots, tramping down the jetty and whistling. Jenny had an elaborate excuse ready but they simply nodded to her as they uncoiled the ropes and let her embark. She bought a day return from the younger ferryman who smiled at her from behind his mask while the older one regarded her carefully as she walked past him down into the seated area.

'Has he got Paul's number?' said Cleo who had managed to poke her head out as Jenny sat on a wooden bench, feeling its glossy varnish under her hands, and breathing in the familiar air of the cabin's interior.

'Yes,' said Jenny. 'But it would take him two hours to get here.'

'And we'll be gone by then?'

Jenny nodded as the ferry's engine roared into life. Sea spray spotted the thick windows as the small boat started to cut across the ripples of the sea loch. She watched Paul's house come into focus on the far shore.

When the ferry docked at the pier she climbed out and, head down, walked quickly past two waiting islanders. On a grassy knoll by the old red phone box, which usually housed cakes and an honesty box, Jenny watched as they disappeared into the boat and the vessel puttered back out into the crossing, leaving a fan of white ruffles trailing after it. Sunlight cracked its way through cloud cover and there was the pip-pip call of some oystercatchers, guarding their nest by the stony beach.

'You can see seals sometimes,' said Jenny, pointing to a craggy islet in the sea. 'One time we watched porpoises, diving up and down out the water.'

'Big whoop,' said Cleo.

The house was the first one at that end of the island, on a small rise facing the water. The gate pushed open, catching at the usual spot. The house stood there, blank windows staring back, the once-white walls looking dingy. Jenny glanced up at the roof tiles and wondered how badly they had leaked while there had been nobody there to put out bowls and pans.

The keys were exactly where she expected them to be. As she slotted the backdoor one into the lock and turned it Jenny looked behind as if she expected one of the islanders to be standing there, demanding to know what she was doing, phone pressed to their ear, informing Paul of her unexpected appearance. But they were alone.

Inside the house was deeply quiet, the strands of sunlight filled with dust motes as the air was disturbed. Jenny pulled the doll out of the rucksack and set her to hover mode. As she walked from room to room of the old farmhouse Cleo followed, making disparaging noises.

'Could he not afford carpet?' she asked as Jenny stepped across timeworn floorboards riddled with holes. There was some plaster missing from the wall too, in the hallway by the front door, which Jenny stared at with new eyes. In the living room there was a large ugly stain of rainwater soaked into floorboards under the bay window and the leather couches were decorated with the pale white bloom of mould.

'How shabby chic,' said Cleo.

They moved upstairs, passing the bathroom with its leaky taps and dusty bath and a room full of junk, before reaching the main bedroom. It was just as Jenny remembered it; a postcard-perfect view stretching over the sea loch from the window. The only difference was the absence of a few jars, bottles and other belongings from the chest of drawers; Paul had posted them back in a huge padded parcel. But the blue throw she had found in a department store sale was still on the bed.

'I bought that,' she said, her voice pathetically forlorn.

Cleo tutted and muttered, 'Did we come all this way for a blanket?'

Back downstairs Jenny scanned the bookcases and raked quickly inside sideboards. In the kitchen she opened and closed cupboards, studied the pinboard, rifled through a pile of mail that was sitting on the doormat.

'These facts you are looking for … have you found them?' said Cleo, who was staring at a trail of mouse droppings.

'My mother gave him that for Christmas,' said Jenny, reaching for a blue glass bottle of gin from the shelf of drinks. She pushed it into her rucksack.

'Technically that's stealing,' said Cleo.

'I don't care,' said Jenny. 'Nothing about his shitty decision was fair. I don't feel the need to play nice.'

'Hence why we are in his house illegally, breaking several laws *and* travel restrictions. My programming has not anticipated these infractions.'

Cleo spun in a slow circle, taking in the kitchen with

its decrepit cooker, threadbare lino and worn units. 'What was so good about him anyway?'

Jenny froze as if ice water had been tipped down her back. He was just a person, but he had been her person. There had been laughter, excitement, the thrill of everything being new and there to be explored, shared. There had been togetherness, whispers in the dark, thoughtful gestures. Until there wasn't any more. There had been a slow fade, a dwindling of the specialness, a feeling that she was being discarded. But the whole world had been in flux; Jenny had thought that if she just hung on it would all come good again.

And then there was the island. It was a long land of green grass, full of bleating lambs in spring, the fields and verges filled with wildflowers and sunlight in summer. It was built of limestone, the old kilns still scattered around the island, the beaches crammed with rocks decorated with white stripes and zigzags and whorls. It was a collision of sky and sea and ancient earth; a place of history, stories, somewhere liminal.

'Do you miss the island more than you miss him?' said Cleo and Jenny wondered if she might vomit again.

On top of the microwave sat two pottery mugs. 'We used to have breakfast in bed,' she muttered, picking them up and turned them around in her hands. Then Jenny found herself moving out the back door, out the gate, across the narrow road and standing on the edge of the slope to the pebble beach. Cleo followed her, a tiny electronic whine filling the air.

'Take that,' said Jenny as she lobbed one of the mugs forwards and watched it smash into pieces among the limestone pebbles. Somewhere further along the beach the oystercatchers squeaked with ferocity.

'A bit childish,' said Cleo.

Jenny stared over the water. There was a gentle slap of seaweed caught on rocks as a tear coursed down her cheek.

'You do know,' said Cleo, 'that he was allowed to end a relationship he didn't want to be in anymore?'

There was a heartbeat when Jenny stood statue-still. Then she launched the second mug in a smooth arc through the air and watched as it cracked into smithereens on the rocks.

For a long heavy silence Jenny breathed in the island air. Then, 'Let's go,' she said in a small voice.

'That's it? Do you feel better now? I mean, we could have smashed some plates at home,' said Cleo as she followed Jenny who was stomping back into the house.

Jenny grabbed her rucksack from where she left it, the bottle of gin bumping and rolling against her back. Then suddenly she was outside while Cleo was still inside, turning round and struggling to orientate herself. Jenny was turning the key in the back door as Cleo hovered into sight at the window. She clattered her small body up against the window pane and mouthed soundless protests as Jenny walked backwards and gave her a small wave. Then she strolled back to the rise above the beach. The ferry was making its way back across the sea loch, a banner of white waves unfurling itself behind it. She took one last long look at the island. Then she hurled the keys down onto the pebbles to lie beside the broken pottery before she walked along the shoreline towards the pier.

An Open Garden
James Mason

AFTERWARDS, DOMINIC WILL drive Connie's Mother home, a quiche congealing on the back seat. Connie will stack the dishwasher and walk between the white plastic tables, throwing the paper plates and cups into a recycling bag.

Before that happens though, Dominic and Connie will stand side by side staring at what's left of the buffet. Amongst the bent tinfoil plates and ricks of wilting cress, there will be rows of cucumber sandwiches, stacked on their trays like shark's teeth, and sausage rolls that have been cut the length of a thumb between nail and second joint, the pastry wet with grease.

One or the other will put their hands on their hips, puff out their cheeks and say in a tired voice that it's a shame to see all this food go to waste.

'All that effort, but I guess it was worth it,' the other will say.

'Well, as long as everyone enjoyed themselves.'

'Yes, I think everyone left suitably happy.'

'Deborah,' Dominic will shout to Connie's Mum, who is in the kitchen. 'Pop the kettle on, would you?'

As it is late in the afternoon, the buffet table will cast a shadow that falls at a long, tipsy angle, leaning away from the couple. Connie will shiver and Dominic reach up and put his hand on her shoulder and they will forget how, earlier that day, rushing to remove a batch of those same sausage rolls, Dominic accidentally presses his thumb against the hot edge of the oven. He will shout 'Fuckingbitchfuckshit,' and drop the tray, sending the sausage rolls scattering all over the laminate floor.

Connie will dash over from where she is slicing cucumbers into weeping, translucent circles and try to hold his hand under the cold tap. Dominic will pull away and suck at the bullet-shaped burn, where a blister is already rising.

In a sharp, accusing tone, he will say 'I'm doing it, OK.'

Connie will go upstairs, take ten deep breaths and sit down to reapply her make up. Only then will she realise that she is still holding the paring knife she had been using to slice the cucumber. Coming up from the kitchen will be the sound of Dominic throwing sausage rolls onto a serving tray.

Connie's Mum will pretend not to hear any of this, instead she will glare more intently at the photograph she picks up, turning the frame over and, using her nail, begin to pick the barcode label off the back.

Between these two events, they'll have the party. Connie will wear a long summer dress patterned with large, vivid thistle heads, that run from her collar bone, over her belly and legs. She will like the way the dress pushes her bust up and that the blue flowers match her eyes. She'll be obliquely proud that, although it rained that morning, all afternoon it will be sunny and the clouds only high and thin and pulled apart. The sunlight will catch her hair in a certain way and make it glow the luminescent blonde it does in the picture she has of herself aged twenty.

Dominic will pour everyone's drinks, then spend twenty minutes walking between the groups of guests. He will clutch a wine bottle in each fist and repeat the mantra 'top up? Top up?' Before the guests arrived, he will have run an extension cord out from the garage and sat their stereo on a card table, where it can provide a constant background of that timid, flavourless jazz people use to paper over the gap between complaints about the roadworks on the bypass and someone else asking about the school's recent Ofsted.

Connie's Mum will talk at great length to a man she thinks might be Connie's Boss, but she isn't sure. To hide her ignorance, she will talk too much, then think she sounds like a wittering old fool, drying up midsentence so the two of them stare in silence at a patch of startled looking delphiniums.

While this is happening, Dominic will use some pre-text to invite Connie's Best Friend into the house and, in the downstairs loo, will drag her dress up over her hips, letting his hands rasp up and down her tights. Connie's Best Friend will say 'No, we can't.' As he slides his hand further up to brush against the cotton of her underwear, he'll feel the place where he burned his thumb as a mysterious, erotic ache. Five minutes after this, they'll emerge out onto the garden again, blinking against the light while he says in a voice that sounds too actorly that after six months the glazing pays for itself.

A little while after Dominic comes back into the garden, Connie will slip away from the party and sit on the bed in the spare room, feeling as if she is trespassing somehow in the room's silence. She'll take a photo of herself, holding the phone above her face, the way mermaids hold mirrors in children's books. The quality of her smile will change and she will pull her dress off her shoulders and lie down on the counterpane, careful to make sure her hair fans out. She'll pout and take several more shots, turning her chin to the left then right, careful to keep the skin on her neck pulled tight. She'll sit up and right her dress and scroll through the image reel, select the one she likes, send it, then delete it along with all the rest. Outside, the man who is talking to Connie's Mum will pull a rueful face and reach for his phone. The man, who might be Connie's Boss, will cough, colour rising up his cheeks and apologise, saying 'Sorry, I have to take this,' then disappear into the house.

Six hours before this, Connie's Mum is in the passenger seat of the car telling her daughter if she really feels this way, there's no reason she has to keep pretending.

Six months after the garden party, the removals men will shift the fridge and find two sausage rolls, furry and all most unidentifiable, coated as they are with mould.

Grit

Jess Moody

THEY ALL WAITED. Buildings hung framed in tasteful monochrome, restrained here on the tenth floor. Kay heard the indignant whispers behind the glass (to be *flattened?*). She understood, but offered no comfort. Pretended not to hear. No one on this earth could beat her for a poker-face.

Her palms rested on the table, where they would leave no sweaty prints, despite her nerves. Her handshake left only gravel-rash, and frowns of concern.

Seated opposite, Ben smoothed his tie with long, blonde-haired fingers. The others tapped patterns, thumbed phones, swung their chairs.

'Christ, how much longer?'

'He'll not be on "coffees" yet.' A 'drinky drinky' mime. Sniggers.

The banter bounced over her. She was a discard, a leftover (in so many ways). Inherited from the multiple mergers, and ill at ease in this new practice, with its pace, its tone, its ambition. Partners moving fast in preparation for long early retirements, young things searching for celebrity over legacy. Architectural *design* they insisted. Free from old structures, no plodding and fussing. *Dynamic.*

She often imagined Joanie here, the pursing of her mentor's eighties-red lips, the hooded-eyes glaring. She'd worked so hard to teach Kay those old ways. After they had … met, Joanie had urged patience. Talked her through the frustration of working on two dimensional surfaces; first paper, then the screens. Smuggled her into an office, a team small and safe and precise. A basement desk. To put her at ease. So far from these glass walled offices, the brochures boasting of designing *spaces* and *lifestyles,* not buildings. She swallowed her scorn at their naiveté. Days and years passed by in compromise.

Now noise and shuffles and heys and hellos as Rob finally entered, warmed with his long lunch, thick with comfort.

'Righto my children, let's fix this fuck-up, shall we?'

The gallery development was in trouble. Ideas faltered back and forth as the Client questioned, wavered; uncertain of her new venture into the Art world (following the short-lived fashion line, jewellery business, and modelling career). The Client was the wife of a certain Somebody, and the practice was keen to please her, without feeling the need to respect her.

'Kay. Go.'

37

She was the one who'd made time with the woman. Explaining, discussing. No judgements for her lack of understanding. Knowledge was just the trick of connecting neurons, yet few here seemed able to master such soft matter (imaginary Joanie shook her head, apologising, again, for the body that failed her. A tar-lunged grunt of guilt).

The Client had stood with Kay in the gaping space behind the historic Kensington frontage, explaining her dreams, her hopes, her fears of it all crumbling (a marriage? A career? A resurrection?). Kay listened. Found a way through. But it would mean delays: to completion, to the final payment, the latest award nomination.

'With this. And this. And this *here*, we can rebalance the space between the main gallery and the private exhibits.' She felt the grind of Rob's jaw as she presented her case. Her deep voice brought frowns to foreheads. She was petite and not a little bony: they expected her to chirrup and flutter. Such poor understanding of density.

'The Client,' she said, 'now feels the current plans suggest restriction, not flow–'

No-one attempted to conceal their eye-rolls.

'– and she's not wrong.'

She made the effort at an encouraging smile. Joanie winked, thumbs up, mouthed *Oh. Kay.*

'I recommend we –'

'Yep, exactly!'

Ah. Ben. Again. The confidence of generations content in their place atop the monument. Clients were reassured by the lie of a tie, the just smoothed vowel sounds, the unapologetic handshake. He had cultivated a habit of taking a long breath in at the start of a sentence, creating a vacuum into which his words would land cleanly.

'So.' Pause. Breath. 'I'm just thinking out loud...But. I reckon Kay may have touched on something there, something that's reminding me of the work I did on the Anderson build.'

He placed a finger humbly on his lips, allowing the name-drop from the practice's prize-winning project to linger.

'I'm thinking, let's take that, and with a bit of work to *mature* the idea –'

Oh.

'– I could see a great opportunity for us. I'm confident I could develop a design that really *chimes* with the Client's overall vision, and of course our *longer-term* practice mission.'

She'd been thinking too small then. So good to have someone with a wider perspective. Joanie shrugged her years-dead shoulders. *Colour me unsurprised.*

Kay kept her hands on the table, seeking stillness in the wood veneer. Finding only the tap tap vibration of Rob's fingers as he mused. Then the nod.

'Great catch Ben, thanks for stepping up.' An unsubtle adjustment to a waistband. 'Kay, let's let Ben progress this, so we can, ah, use you elsewhere. Moving on…'

A triumphant flicker in Ben's eyes, before carefully avoiding her gaze. Months they'd been working on this together, and this is the story that would be told.

She had hoped this time it would be different. She'd stepped out of her usual isolation. Tried to make them see. Perhaps, too, she'd been not a little inspired by the Client herself, shedding skins with each metamorphosis, a pursuit of self-definition.

The agenda moved on, formed and reformed, the dull reverberation of young ambition. Kay's attention sank through her palms, seeking a balance; down beyond the table-top, through into the legs, the carpet of plastic. She found concrete floors branching off the central stairwell, the illusion of solidity.

A rare sense of vertigo.

She sat until the talking stopped, and the room emptied of colleagues and ghosts. She felt the buildings in the photographs watching her. Waiting. She pushed their judgement away, down.

Ten floors below, cracks in the concrete spidered out in rings.

SHOW-TIME, JOANIE WHISPERED, before vanishing again.

She'd felt further away these past months.

Ben and the Client stepped over the threshold first. The woman's heels caught for a second on the ruched-up plastic sheeting over the floorboards – Ben's hand remained hovering at her elbow at a faux-deferential distance. It hadn't taken long for him to find a way to secure Kay's help without conceding his need. Hints were dropped about prioritisation, support, not being overly sensitive. A team player. She assisted quietly, diligently. Now, trailing behind, she paused to close the heavy door to the street, shutting out the afternoon sun, the thrum of diesel.

Hello. She gave greetings, her hand on the doorframe. The building stood without comment, a supposedly indifferent old relation. She carried on through the foyer.

Entering the main gallery space, its double height ceiling dwarfing tools and dust-sheets, she could see all was not well. The Client wore a frozen kind of smile, a furrow at the top of her carefully sculpted nose. She was turning slowly, refocusing her mismatched expectations. Ben, in panic, talked too much.

'As you can see, they're very much on track, and the changes, the most recent changes you very carefully deliberated over, are, I hope, in keeping with our earlier discussions.'

The latest developments had been his suggestion. Rushed, selfish, an uncomfortable warping of Kay's plan.

He had wanted to push for something sharper, something for awards season, his portfolio. Too much had been stripped. The space left empty, neutered, cornices smoothed, floors levelled, everything, everything white.

Ben turned back to her, a mix of frustration, contempt, and questioning: *why is this woman not satisfied?*

She sensed this was a question he was not used to asking.

Between them she felt the building's smirk. It had been dug up and sawed and drilled and polished and painted by rough uncaring hands, and remained utterly unmoved by any desire to welcome its inhabitants.

They'd failed. In the smell of paint and sawdust, and the distant echo of traffic, they could all see it. Perhaps the Client would be grudgingly convinced. There would be a successful launch, the floors would be baptised with spilt prosecco and stiletto heels, dropped plates and secret cigarettes. But soon the art would hang in a sterile space. The visitors would venture in, tempted by the outward age and whimsy. They'd make a polite circuit, no privacy in the reverberations of their whispers, and exit swiftly as if to a forgotten appointment. Staff would sneak out before shift-end for the warmth of nearby coffee-shops. In a year, the business would barely break even, accumulating only the fingerprints smudges of glass and steel. As for the building, it would sit, a shell once more, awaiting its next surgery or demolition. The development of select luxury residential apartments would soon call. More work, perhaps, for the practice.

Ben ushered the Client into the back rooms, words of reassurance bouncing around, failing to make any purchase.

Kay stayed. Placed her forehead to the cool concrete wall, splayed her fingers in load-bearing prayer. Her face indicated a respectful question, a search.

Lean in, the room snickered. She hunted on.

There. There was the problem. And there. Too many extractions, corners unloved and beams removed. *The light.* The sun from the high windows no longer flowed off and round surfaces, or flattered solid form with shadow and gleam. No kiss of heat and truth. Instead, only diffused nothingness. One little change had tilted everything out of balance: a cascade of hollowed hopes.

Closing her eyes, she reached into the walls. Round the beams and blocks, inching around the stone and the mortar and the brick and the glass. She felt the warmth of the winter sun on the building's front.

Work with me here, she said. She offered salvation – for the building, for her career. As Joanie had once offered to her.

The negotiation was slow. Battered and bruised, the internal fixtures were reluctant to move again. Stubborn. She pleaded for her generation, imposed the guilt of the needy relative. The foundations leant their strength, and the city rumbled on, and it was the work of moments to shift a few inches here, compress a few millimetres there. Wooden doors and frames creaked like the dead things they were. The walls sighed soft plaster dust, a last grumble of compressed air.

She coughed, inhaling grit and splinters, eyeing the new angles with satisfaction. The light took in subtly new surfaces, filled forgotten corners with warmth, and played with the patterns of the picture rails. Here was what a building could be, should be. All would be well.

'Vozje moy!' She froze at the sight of the Client in the doorway. The tall woman took slow steps back into the middle of the room, Ben stumbling out from behind her, rattled. He frowned slightly at a new crack along a wall, stared at the just-trembled floor, but she knew he was incapable of *seeing*. Of feeling how things were made for themselves.

The Client spun with her hands to her cheeks, squeezing her smile between them.

'I was not sure somehow but now … now I see. It is perfect! Thank you, Benjamin, and, yes, Kay, thank you!'

Ben quickly assumed his confident smile and submitted to her praise. Neither of them looked at her again.

THE EMAIL DEMANDED the attendance of the whole Practice. The briefing room. High noon. The partners hovered at the head of the table, leaving the seats free for the junior staff. The atmosphere one of parents graciously attending the Christmas play. A bucket of champagne sweated.

Rob came and leaned against the wall near her, crossed his arms lazily. Nodded briefly to his team. To Ben, in his matching tie.

'Right everyone, settle down now.' The senior partner.

Licked lips, skirts smoothed under the desk, backs straightened. Brace, brace.

The pre-amble. The practice's commitment to innovation. The delight of a certain Client, and naturally, haha, her husband's relief at her delight. The husband, whose identity surely everyone is now aware of. High Net Worth. The hint of more work. Lucrative work. Yet, the importance of rewarding care, and dedication to shaping a client's vision. A true meritocracy: the celebration of major new talent.

'Ben, would you come up here?'

His faux surprise. Her sense of being tipped.

The applause rang round. Mostly genuine. They'd heard. The gallery *had* been special. A persistent buzz about its 'surprising' warmth and personality. Such an empathetic reimagining. Articles in trade press had been promised, accolades hinted.

Kay sat with her hands still, feeling her face stiffen.

She knew what would follow. Promotion, awards for him. Privilege building on privilege as he soared amongst the buzz and the noise and the suits and the success. She would stay, precarious, wavering.

Rob's voice in her ear was an oily murmur.

'Now, now Kay, don't begrudge your colleague his success. Show your appreciation, please.'

She turned. He nodded down at her still hands. Nervous glances from the others as the applause rang on, whoops as bubbles surged.

She shut her eyes. Another year. Another year. The crumble, and the wear.

No.

She reached.

Leapfrogging the floors, finding the paving and asphalt. Deeper, along tunnels, feeling the violence of cobbles cleansed of protest, a city built on clay and not a little ash.

'Kay?'

Out to where the river fought the embankments for its ancient right of way. The comfort of the skeleton of structures above her, beside her, within, holding the mess of humanity together. The memory of many hands making out of the earth their own dream of safety. The noise and the cold and the heat and the endless, endless patience.

'Kay, c'mon now.' A hiss, saliva inadvertently on her

neck. 'Don't be a *child.*'

She found everything made from the hard, watching earth. Took the north and the south of the city in each hand and held them tight.

Build something better they whispered as they gripped on, weighty and waiting. She opened her eyes, looked around the room, and smiled at Joanie's proud nod.

She was made for this.

With the city in her hands – she clapped.

Self-archaeology
Juana Riepenhausen

YOU ASK ME how they got away with it. Easy: we travelled light. My mum would carry passports and documents in her purse, my dad packed a carry-on suitcase for the clothes we would need on our first week. On arrival, we went on a shopping spree to fill my wardrobe with colourful leggings and cosy sweaters. When it was time to move again, I would roll my Jurassic Park poster – the only belonging I was allowed to take with me – and secure it with a scrunchy, as my mum put all my stuff into bags and took them to the local church. If I cried, she would call me selfish. Other kids didn't have food, let alone my endless possibilities. If you grew up looking out the same window year after year, wishing you could run free, drown your envy. I would've personally preferred to own a bed frame decorated with sparkly stickers I could one day peel off to wave my childhood goodbye. The grass is always greener and all that jazz.

The corners of my precious poster were weak from so much sticking and unsticking tape onto them, so I resorted to throwing tantrums and asking for it to be framed. Claiming that glass was both weak and heavy, inconvenient for our lifestyle, my parents repeatedly refused to do it. I refused to give in. Caught in a hurricane of fleeting moments, this fight was the only constant I could hold on to. My mother was a longshot, but I knew dad would eventually yield. This was the least he could do – his words, not mine. By the time he did frame it, I must have been around eight and we were already in our sixth house that would never be a home. I could speak Spanish, English and French. I had never had a birthday party.

I don't recall Buenos Aires, despite it being my place of birth. According to my passport, we didn't stay anywhere for more than six months, skipping across Uruguay, Peru, Colombia, Mexico. Stamp, stamp, stamp. Canada was where I lived for the longest time before finishing primary school; a year and a half in total. I believe it was in Montreal where my dad taught me how to make a snowman. Following an uncharacteristic desire to respect institutions, he used a carrot for the nose. I'd show you a picture, but there are none. I am a photographer raised by parents who never owned a camera. Call it ironic or predictable. I used to think it was romantic, but that was before I realised my life revolves around making up for lost time.

There isn't any evidence that I existed before the age

of fifteen. No pictures, no records, not even friends. It would be a miracle to find a classmate who remembers me, having left no trace behind. I like to think I was a funny little comedian, but surely my unforgettable yet faceless jokes have now been attributed to someone more memorable. I don't think it's self-centred of me to resent this. You would also fight for remembrance, oblivion hurts more than just your ego. We are the memories we imprinted on others. If they go missing, we follow suit. For some months now, I have been feeling like a water hyacinth, endlessly floating. I long to find the roots of my true self, a blueprint to reconstruct my essence, an inner child who knows my soul and could show me where to go next. I barely know that girl and can't even picture her face, so I guess I am condemned to keep digging for fossils I will never find.

Even though I never had one taken, I knew what a photo was. I occasionally went to friends' houses and saw their portraits beaming from numerous frames. The only frame we owned was the one that displayed my poster. The thing that excited me the most about staying in Canada for a full school year was the possibility of appearing in the annual group picture and finally seeing my face staring back at me from a glossy piece of paper. I knew my mother wouldn't wake up early to braid my hair, so I spent a month practising in front of the mirror to master the technique. My short fingers weren't the best tools I could've asked for, but I was nonetheless happy with the results. When I woke up that morning, I noticed it was too bright, too late. I found my mum in bed, reading a book. She said my father had taken the car and left for work early, so she had let me skip school. By now, I had learnt there was no use in causing a scene if he wasn't around, so I turned back, ignoring her indifference. You can't say ours wasn't a reciprocal relationship.

My mum died of cancer without ever loving me. You ask me to be less blunt, I tell you to get over it. One can't spend eternity avoiding the obvious. Now that people know my story, I have been told that the stubbornness with which she decided to despise me, a child that was too scared to do something wrong, should have raised some alarms. I guess nobody was paying that much attention. I do feel sorry for her – she would've hated the flatness that has been bestowed upon her by the media. I shall never defend her but I will say this: my mother was a complex woman, she had layers. I am personally fascinated by the consistency with which she kept me near only so I could see the hatred in her eyes from up close. I know that before she died, in the silence of her last days, she smiled as she caressed my dad's hand and gloated thinking her rejection had ruined my life. Imagine hating someone with such intention, just so you can flatter yourself. I wish I could say she got it wrong, but the echoes of her treatment are plastered on my demeanour like ugly tattoos. You wouldn't ask what they mean, nobody does. I guess people think I'm just bad-tempered, and maybe I am. Do I sound angry to you?

You ask me why I prefer to talk about my mum. Simple: because it's easier, cleaner, sharper. Things get tricky when I talk about my dad. He did what he did and you can't deny it (believe me, I've tried), but he would also dry my ears when I left the shower and wrap me in a towel to turn me into a burrito. So what do you make of that? What do you make of him?

After Canada, Portugal and Spain, I passed through France, Russia and I finally spent some time in Norway. I wouldn't personally recommend it, the cold kills. Figuratively speaking in my case, but it killed my dad for real. Now it has been two years since I got back to Buenos Aires. My dad had never allowed me to return. He used to say South America had become too dangerous in the last decades. Ignoring the feeling of betrayal, I bought the ticket. When you have no family left, the need for belonging gets as piercing and sharp as a toothache. Thoughts zigzag without clarity until you do something about it. Going to the city where I had been born seemed like a sensible solution, but I was wrong. I didn't understand the jokes about TV personalities, and when I tried to use slang it sounded as if I had been practicing the words. I'm grateful that he's dead. It would break his heart to see that us, citizens of the world, are just people without a home. The idea of him being hurt still feels unbearable.

You already know the rest. I found Mercedes as she was leaving the supermarket. Actually, she found me. I don't think you can properly find something you didn't know you were supposed to be searching for. I always call her Mercedes when she isn't around. The second time we talked she asked me to start calling her Mum, and I agreed to it because I'm afraid she will get impatient if I don't. Mum. It's weird. The word always had such a horrible taste in my mouth. My mum thought I was a freak. My mum died of cancer. My mum never loved me.

I call her Mum and she calls me Celeste, the name she chose when she had me. I don't like it, but I let her get away with it because she's been through a lot. Technically I have too, but I don't see it that way. I had no knowledge of her existence and, in spite of everything, my dad was an excellent father. Mercedes keeps asking questions about him, but I excuse myself claiming that it's hard to go there. My theory is that, if I bring him back to life, she will notice how much I take after him, the mystery man, the villain, the monster. I'm not ready to lose her too.

It didn't take her long to convince me her story was also mine. Seeing my eyes in her face was proof enough. Everything that came after that has been a little bit overwhelming for my liking: crying strangers touching me, entire folders containing old newspaper cutouts, thin needles promising certainties. Both Mercedes and I know the most important question will remain unanswered forever. I tell her about stolen phrases I caught falling from my parents' mouths, just in case she can give them meaning. It's pointless. We will never know why he chose me, I will never know why he allowed himself to die without giving up the truth.

According to Mercedes, it happened at the cinema. These things were not strange in the nineties, which is why she had specifically asked Roberto—her dead husband and in theory my dad—to keep an eye on my sister and me. She tells the story with plenty of details to check if I recall something, but all I can do is stare into her eyes that haven't stopped crying since she found me two months ago. The scene is displayed in separate photograms that I can't put in motion to wake up something in my memory. First comes my sister running to get popcorn and tripping over her shoelaces, then Mercedes dashing to help her, leaving me next to Roberto, who stayed for too long looking at the Jurassic Park poster, bigger than the one I was holding in my hand. Apparently this is when my dad—the only dad I'll ever have—enters the scene, takes me into his arms and hides me inside his jacket, taking me away from my family, claiming me as his child, forever sentencing me to be a wound I ignored I was, a girl without a name, an open sea between two coasts: that in which I hate him for what he did and the one where I still find myself hugging his memory.

You ask me how I am coping and I tell you I'm not. All I have ever been is his making. Lacking nature, his nurture shaped me. And the knowledge of what he's done has erased the certainty of who he was. I ask you: how do you know how to grow, if you don't recognise the seed you came from?

You ask me how I keep loving him, even now. I tell you: reluctantly, daily. Tell me what you make of that. Please, tell me what you make of me.

Stuck for Words
Iqbal Hussain

I DIDN'T KNOW who the elderly man was. Mother had left me with him in the front room, which was normally reserved for visitors. I perched on a pouffe, while the stranger reclined on the sofa. With his crocheted *topi*, prayer beads and flowing, henna-stained beard, he looked like an exotic Santa Claus.

Avoiding his gaze, I made a show of taking in the furnishings: the settee with its plastic cover to preserve the fabric; the Taj Mahal table; the starburst clock hanging above a mirror festooned with peacock feathers, fake jewellery and wedding invites.

The man gave a big sniff. I looked round – he was snorting snuff, taking a generous pinch from a little tin. As he crossed his legs, he nearly slid off the sofa, his cotton *salwar kameez* struggling to make a purchase on the plastic. I tried not to laugh. Harrumphing, he righted himself and fixed me with a gimlet stare. '*Achha – kya baath hai, beta?*'

Although we spoke Punjabi at home, I was familiar

with Urdu as it was similar to the Hindi of Bollywood films. 'The m-m-m-matter? N-n-n-nothing, s-s-s-sir,' I replied in English. The Glitch wasted no time in making itself known. That was what I called my stammer. It was a multi-legged spider in my throat, all spiky and sharp-edged, like something drawn by Zorro's sword.

Not convinced, the old man switched to broken English as though this might bring a different response. 'Hmmmm, nothing? I see, I see. No worry. I hear for myself. Problem in your mouth, hmmm?' He did a head waggle. I raised my eyebrows and stored away the waggle to try out myself later. 'We sort-short you out, *puthar*. Just one, two, three things first.'

Mother bustled in with a rattan *changher* on her head, on which she had a couple of mismatched mugs of cardamom-scented milky tea and a packet of cake rusks still in their box. In her hand, she carried a saucepan. When she put it down, I saw it was full of sultanas, plump from being sautéed in butter. That was a strange thing to serve to a guest, I thought.

'Do you have everything you need, Doctor *saab*?' she asked.

This man was a doctor? He wasn't Dr Khan, our normal GP. Not that I wanted him either – Dr Khan was as warm as a fridge freezer. He'd scowl as you walked into the consulting room, as though you were wasting his time just by being there.

'Fine, fine,' said the orange-bearded one. 'Me and the little boy are getting to knowing each another.' He smiled at Mother and waggled his head once more.

She giggled, uncharacteristically shy, hiding her face behind her *dupatta*. 'I'll leave you to it, Dr Shah.' She left the room backwards, bowing, trailing her trademark scent of Tibet face cream.

'Dr' Shah took a big slurp of tea, smacking his lips, and dunked a rusk in it, demolishing it in three bites. He worked through another couple of rusks, before looking at the half-empty packet as if debating whether to continue. Belching, he rubbed his tummy, then looked at me, as if remembering I was still there. 'One mint, please.'

I wondered where the Polos were, before realising he was saying 'minute'. He opened up a metal box, like the one Father kept his tools in. He began taking out various things: bottles containing liquids; a bunch of dried herbs; a couple of metal serving spoons; and a peg. I looked to the door, but Mother was gone.

'Son, come here.' He patted the sofa, which rustled stickily.

'W-w-w-what for?' I said, reluctant to leave the safety of the pouffe.

'No worry, *beta*, your mummy just ask me to taking a look.'

'A look? At w-w-what?'

He grinned, revealing a snaggle tooth in his upper

jaw. 'Come, come. Sit.'

As I made no sign of moving, he reached over and pulled me up. The unexpectedness of the move meant I flew up and landed on the sofa on my knees. The plastic felt unpleasant against my shorts-clad legs. I'd barely time to rearrange myself before Mr Shah gripped me around the jaw. Before I could protest, he'd shovelled a spoonful of sultanas into my mouth.

'Swallow, *beta*. They will help.'

It was like eating bogeys. The only way I could get them down was without chewing. While I swallowed, Mr Shah kept up a prayer, occasionally blowing the words into my face. Each time I gagged, Mr Shah forced in another spoonful, not stopping until he'd got through the pan.

As expected, I threw up – I felt my stomach buck and heave, and then the sultanas came back up, not too dissimilar in shape to how they'd gone in. Mr Shah seemed prepared for this and held the pan under my mouth, tapping me on the back, encouraging me to get it all out.

'How feel, *beta*?' he asked, when I was finally done.

I grimaced and reached for the flamenco doll on the table, lifting up her skirts for the kitchen roll hidden there. Where was Mother? The door remained shut. Mr Shah looked at me, clearly expecting a reply. I had to wipe the sick off my mouth first. I retched some more. Mr

Shah backed away.

'I d-d-don't like s-s-s-s-sult-t-t-tanas,' I managed, stammering worse than ever. 'And they d-d-d-don't like m-m-m-me.'

Mr Shah set down the pan with a thump on the floor. 'I see. Okay, okay, *puthar*, don't you worry. I fix-fix no problem.'

Waggling his head again, he turned his attention to the serving spoons. Dipping them into a bowl of water, which Mother had brought in earlier, he cupped my head with them. They were cold – I yelped. Ignoring my protests, he began chanting, in what sounded like Arabic. With each new chant, he cupped a different part of my head with the spoons.

After five or so minutes, he put the spoons down. He uncorked one of the bottles and, partially covering the opening with a snuff-greened thumb, shook the bottle over the top of my head as though vinegaring a bag of chips. Cold, sticky drops of liquid peppered my head. The smell of oil filled my nostrils. My fringe began to get slick. I imagined I looked like Carrie in the poster of the film.

Having doused me thoroughly, Mr Shah picked up the spoons once more. This time, he placed them back-to back so that the bowls touched. He then circled my head with them, not touching, just allowing the spoons to clack against each other. Again, more chanting. From next door, I heard *Crackerjack* on the TV and desperately wished I was in there. The smell of *parathas* wafted through the gaps at the top and bottom of the door. My mouth salivated, imagining the crispy, buttery flatbreads.

'How does feel, *puthar*? You notice difference?'

'It f-f-f-feels … sh-sh-sh-should I feel something d-d-d-d-'

The spoons clanged even louder, as did the chanting. The water or oil or whatever he'd poured on my head had made its way down my face now. The dripping liquid tickled my cheeks. I made to wipe it away, but Mr Shah tapped me on the back of the hand with the spoons.

A few moments later, he sighed and laid down the spoons, grabbing my face in his hands. 'Think about Allah, *beta*. Think about mummy. Think about Pakistan, *zinda baad*!'

Mr Shah thumped his chest at this nationalistic exhortation, before picking up the spoons in one hand and the peg in the other. He brought the peg up to my mouth. What was I meant to do with it? I made to take it from him, but he smacked the back of my hand with the spoons. 'Open, *beta*. Tongue out.'

I had no idea what he was doing. But I'd been brought up to respect my elders, so I did as he said, trying not to bring up the sultanas.

Mr Shah pounced. With surprising dexterity, he scissored my tongue between his second and third fingers, sticking the peg on the tip. As I looked at him aghast, pain throbbing through my tongue and the bitter taste of tobacco in my mouth, he waggled his head as this was a perfectly normal turn of events.

He went back to his metal cabinet and pulled out a feather. He stroked my face, focussing on my mouth, circling first clockwise, then anticlockwise. Being ticklish, I could only bear this for a few seconds. I sneezed, sending the peg flying. It landed in Mr Shah's lap.

'Come, come, *beta*,' he chastised. 'This no way behave your olders.'

Once more, the peg went back on the tip of my tongue. Once more, the chanting started up. Once more, the bottle of water began its sprinkling. Once more, the spoons began their noisy journey around my face. Once more, the feather caressed my mouth.

After what seemed like a million years, Mr Shah stopped. I breathed a sigh of relief. But then he picked up the bunch of herbs. Fumbling in a pocket on his *kameez*, he took out a lighter. A pungent smell like the dead cat I'd come across last week on the canalside filled the room. My appetite was instantly suppressed.

Mr Shah seemed oblivious to the smell. Standing up, he wafted the burning herbs around my head, incanting once more. To make sure I got the full effect, he blew the smoke into my face. I coughed and my eyes watered. Once more, I threatened to throw up. Mr Shah poked me with a forefinger. 'Be big boy now.'

Mother knocked on the door and poked her head in. She showed no surprise at seeing my tongue out with a peg on it. 'Would you like to say for biryani, Dr *saab*?'

Mr Shah beamed. 'Yes, yes! Splendid. Nearly done, missus. Two more mints.'

Mother retreated, humming an old Bollywood number.

Mr Shah ended as he'd begun, grabbing my face between his hands, scrutinising it for – well, for heaven knows what. He must have seen something he didn't like, for he picked up the spoons and gave a final clatter in front of my forehead, before cupping my ears and looking intently at my eyes.

'How is feel, *puthar*? Don't be shy. You can telling your uncle.'

I opened my mouth, but instead of words I coughed like my dad's car trying to start on a cold morning, the smoke from the herbs still heavy in the air.

Mr Shah smacked me on the back. 'There, there, let it out. That is just your … your 'thing' saying bye-bye.'

Did he mean my stammer? I coughed some more. Mr Shah was so close to my face I could smell the flowery *attar* he wore. The ticking of the clock filled my ears. From next door came the sound of laughter – the others had switched to BBC2, to watch Harold Lloyd, just before the News.

I tried to talk, but gibberish came out – I still had the

peg on my tongue. Mr Shah tutted and unclipped it. I cleared my throat. 'I think it's –'

'*Wah, wah,*' said Mr Shah, throwing his hands up at the apparent miracle of my newfound fluency after hearing just three small words. He got up with a crick-crack of his knees. 'Come, let us eat some *taazi-taazi* biryani. Your mummy is good cooker, no?'

I followed him out, none the wiser from what had passed. I smelt like a bonfire and my tongue hurt. A taste of butter and bile coated my mouth and throat.

The only thing I was certain about was that Mr Shah's witch-doctor quackery had had zero effect on my stammer. The Glitch was still in my throat. It taken one look at Mr Shah's paraphernalia and thrown open its zigzag mouth in glee. Its shoulders pumped up and down, like the birds in *Roobarb and Custard*.

The Leonids
Paul J. Jackson

November, 1833.

IT WAS A cold sharp, moonless, night. Bobby, the farmer's son, had just locked the large shires into their stalls when a strange noise caught his attention. It was coming from outside the barn and he ran into the yard to investigate. His eyes were instantly drawn to the heavens.

The night sky appeared to be on fire as streams of light darted across it. Bobby could hear them blazing through the atmosphere like rockets. There were so many that it was impossible to count them and they lit up the yard enough for him to see clearly.

Before long his father, Jack, and sister, Maisie, had joined him. Their eyes too were fixed on the blazing sky, awestruck and frightened. The bright projectiles were flying in all directions and many appeared to be falling to earth.

Small rocks began to bounce off the dirt around them. One or two at first, falling randomly here and there, but the frequency quickly built. Worried for their safety, Jack ushered his family into the cellar below the farmhouse. It was cold and dark but at least they were safe.

After several attempts with his Lucifer matches, Jack eventually lit an old lamp. His son and daughter huddled up to it as they listened to the falling rocks smash the windows above them and clatter off the farmhouse roof and cellar doors.

The blazing sky had frightened Maisie, but she was more afraid of the pelting chunks of icy rock than the fizzing stars. She struggled to make sense of it all.

'Is God angry with us, father?' she asked as she sat on the floor dithering in the darkness.

Jack looked down at her. At fourteen, Maisie had begun to blossom into a young lady. She was a little too thin for his liking and far too self-conscious about her appearance. The boys in town were beginning to notice her and he knew that one day soon one of those lads would come a calling. But, as she looked up at him through the glimmering lamp light, all he could see was a petrified little girl.

'Nay, child,' he replied reassuringly, as he continued to watch the bizarre sky show through the planks of the cellar doors, 'They're shooting stars is all.'

His mind was thrown back thirty years or so to when he was a lad of around twelve. He remembered there being a similar event on another cold November evening. He recalled how scared he was and how his mother had also assumed that it must be the work of God.

After losing his wife, Mary-Beth, Jack had turned his back on faith. He had prayed in vain for her to get well but she eventually died a long and painful death. In his eyes her misery had been prolonged to spite him.

The shower of falling rocks had begun to peter out. They had not been as bad as Jack had feared and he sensed that soon they would be able to return to the house. He could only hear a few hitting the roof tiles now and the sound of breaking glass had stopped.

However, as he put his hand to the cellar door, a thunderous roar startled him and saw the sky was on fire through the warped planks. A second later the ground shook as something big hit the land nearby. A shower of choking dust, dislodged from the floorboards above as the farmhouse juddered, rained down on them. Unable to breathe they were forced to emerge from the cellar for air.

Jack led them up onto the open porch beneath the canopy. The whizzing display overhead still lit up the night sky but the intensity had waned. Bobby and his sister stared at the sky rockets in awe but, Jack's eyes were focussed elsewhere. He had spotted a faint glow coming from the woods.

It was too dark for him to judge the distance but he knew that, whatever it was, had just caused the ground to quake and forced them from the cellar. It had to be a meteorite and he felt compelled to investigate.

Bobby glanced at his father and his eyes were drawn towards the distant glow.

'What is it father?' he asked, stepping closer.

'A meteorite, I guess,' replied Jack.

'Can we go see?'

Jack glanced down at Maisie for a moment before looking back at the orange haze through the trees. His daughter was afraid and he felt inclined to wait until first light.

'It will look better at night,' added Bobby, as if reading his father's mind.

Jack turned to face him and smiled. At sixteen, his son was almost as tall as he was. He was no longer a child and Jack knew that Bobby would end up going there by himself as soon as his back was turned. The boy had inherited his streak of adventure and, once he had set his mind on something, nothing could stop him.

He had to agree with Bobby. The red hot meteorite would look more impressive at night. By day it would just be a smouldering lump of ash. Now the small rocks had stopped falling it would be safe to venture out.

Jack sent Bobby for the lamp in the cellar while he and Maisie went back into the house for their coats and a second lamp. Before leaving, Jack grabbed his percussion cap pistol, some shot and a powder bag. It was dark out and he had heard talk of wolves in the area.

It was biting cold on the open pasture but, with the

sky on fire and two lamps, at least they could see where they were walking. Before too long they had reached the perimeter of the wood. The glow was a few hundred yards into the trees but already they could see the path it had taken through them.

It had completely ripped the canopy off several trees and the further they ventured in the lower to the ground the destruction got until, eventually, the trees were replaced by scorched bare earth.

At last, the glowing rock was no more than twenty or thirty feet in front of them and they stood staring at the devastation it had caused. The meteorite was sat at the end of a large crater with the gouged earth piled up behind it.

Bobby stepped closer but his father held him back. There was something about the large rock that made him wary. He was no expert when it came to space rocks but, even he knew that the shape and size of this one was odd.

Old man Jefferson in the village had a small collection of space debris on display at the back of his news stand. The largest rock was the size of a fist but all the samples were rough and jagged. Some were a little rounded, after being burned up in the atmosphere but, even they were misshapen. The large rock before him however was massive, egg shaped and almost perfectly smooth. He knew that its appearance would not have occurred naturally.

It was standing upright in its crater and the earth around it was smouldering. The glow they had seen in the distance had come from the felled trees and branches. Some were still on fire but most had reduced to huge glowing embers, crackling and popping as they pulsed with heat.

Maisie, who had been dragged there against her will, was also wary of the strange monolith. She yanked at her father' sleeve and begged to be taken home.

With his pistol poised, Jack edged towards it, slipping from Maisie's grip. Bobby began to follow behind but his father ordered him to stay put.

'Let me check it first, son,' he added, entering the crater.

He could feel his boots warming from the smouldering soil under foot but the heat was bearable. He traversed the incline and as he neared the meteorite he was able to see more detail.

It stood about nine feet tall with a diameter of around six feet. It was dark grey in colour and perfectly symmetrical. The surface resembled that of pumice, like solidified froth made from tiny air bubbles. It looked quite smooth but Jack could tell it would feel rough to the touch.

Cautiously, he stretched out his hand and, surprised that it generated no heat, he eventually placed his finger tips against it. It was cold and rock hard. He had expected the surface to crumble, or shed off like loose sand, but the material was unyielding.

Bobby called to his father. He wanted to join him but was told to keep his distance for now. The lad walked to the edge of the crater for a closer look.

Brushing his hand across the surface, Jack began to circle the object. He had only taken two or three steps when he came across a vertical slit running down the side. The cut was perfectly straight and seemed to encompass the monolith as it continued over the top. He made his way to the other side to check.

Sure enough, the incision encircled the stone precisely and Jack stepped back. His first thought had been correct. This thing was not natural. It had been designed and made by someone and sent to earth for a reason.

Jack could now see a fine mist seeping from the slit and his ears were picking up a subtle hissing sound. The crackling embers of the trees and branches that surrounded the pit made it difficult to hear at first but the noise soon got louder as the mist turned to steam.

Realising the object was about to crack open, Jack, darted back up the slope of the crater and stood at the rim pointing his old pistol at it. Maisie ran to his side followed by Bobby. Their father' sudden retreat had made them uneasy.

'What is it, Dad?' Maisie asked, grabbing his hand, 'What's happening?'

Just then another thundering meteorite blazed across

the sky above them and they watched as it disappeared over the trees and out of sight. It was quite high but Jack knew it was going to crash somewhere near the next town, he also felt that it would be identical to the one they had just discovered.

The steam and hissing had now ceased and they watched with trepidation as it began to open, rotating the front half of the shell back into the rear half. The egg shaped craft now had a flat side facing the family and a shimmering centre had been revealed. It pulsed and rippled as though it was breathing.

The family stepped back a little further, Jack ready to shoot with his arm outstretched before him. They watched as the pulsating core began to glow and shimmer like liquid glass before sending out an intense flash of light that flooded the entire woods for just a millisecond.

Dazzled, the family stood staring at the object. The flash was so sudden they had not had time to blink and were now staring at the object as if in a trance. Involuntarily, both Bobby and Maisie dropped their lamps.

Jack lowered his arm and began to approach the craft again followed by his children. He wanted to stop, to tell his kids to stay put, but for some strange and frightening reason he couldn't. The object was pulling them towards it and was controlling their every step.

Maisie began to cry as she realised what was happening. She tried her damndest to resist against it but to no avail. Bobby was struck dumb and simply followed his father into the crater.

As they neared the shimmering screen they could see a figure stood still within it. It was a humanoid, legs, arms, torso but there was no face. Jack approached and stood in front of the rippling figure that now appeared to be waving him in with a fingerless hand.

Jack obliged, dropping his pistol at his feet before stepping through the liquid glass. Bobby and Maisie watched as the rippling figure embraced their father as he entered. The pulsating screen distorted the view but beyond they could see enough to know that the alien inside was now crushing their father to death.

Powerless to run they watched in horror as he struggled free himself before falling lifeless from sight. A second figure appeared and Bobby was next to be beckoned in. He obeyed the unheard command to enter.

Maisie wanted to scream, to flee, but the alien control was too strong. She watched as her brother was crushed to death in the arms of the terrifying figure, knowing that she was next and could do nothing to prevent it.

As Bobby's lifeless body fell out of sight she crossed over into the craft involuntarily, a puppet without strings. She had expected to be covered in liquid as she passed through the screen but was subjected to a wave of intense prickles instead. She was now standing inside a shimmering metallic room and could hear a deep humming sound.

A faceless alien stood before her. It looked almost unfinished; with its blank face, fingerless hands and no genitals. It reminded Maisie of her wooden doll, waiting to be dressed.

She could now see Bobby and her father lying beside each other on the metal floor with the aliens that had killed them kneeling by their sides. They had their fingerless hands over the faces of their victims. The one that had taken her father looked different from the other. It had begun to change, to morph into something else.

It now had a face, hair, fingers and its body was changing shape. Maisie finally screamed as she realised what was happening. The creatures were becoming human, taking the forms of those they had killed.

Suddenly she was grabbed around the waist by the alien that had beckoned her in and it quickly squeezed the air from her lungs as it crushed her to death. As she faded out she could see a mass of unfinished creatures in the background waiting their turn and queuing up towards the shimmering doorway.

JACK, BOBBY AND Maisie stepped from the portal, each inhaling a breath of air into their new lungs as they scanned their surroundings. Their steps were unsteady at first but were soon on their way back to the farmhouse. The leonid meteor shower above had now faded away with the rising sun.

'Hurry!' Jack said, still buttoning his shirt and glancing back at his children, 'We need everyone in town to come and see the meteorite.'

The Lighthouse Keeper's Wife
Helen Chambers

THE MOON SCATTERS pearls on the dancing waves, and I sigh. Ted doesn't hear me, he hasn't heard so well since his last bout of pneumonia. His pen scratches across the lighthouse log book, recording the precise time he rewound the clockwork mechanism, polished the reflector glass of the lantern, exchanged radio messages, observed the safe passage of one of our ships.

Lately I haven't been sleeping, so when he's on duty, I sit beside him in the Service Room near the top of the tower just beneath the lantern gallery. The graveyard shift, midnight until 4am. Tomorrow, my eyes will ache with tiredness, yet I'll be wakeful, even with Ted's snores filling our little cottage, one of three in this lighthouse station compound, across the yard from the tower.

I want to tell him what they said in the butcher's today. But I can't think how to bring it up. It's gossip, I suppose. I mustn't interrupt Ted when he's on duty, so I tuck it away for later. Instead, I listen out for planes.

Even though the lighthouse tower is camouflaged, to

me, we're a sitting duck. Ted reassures me that Lighthouses aren't used by the Military, everyone knows the Geneva Convention, but still, Jerry knows we're here. Blackout or not, we show our light five minutes each hour for our own ships, so our position is clear for anyone who wants to know. Everyone on the station is trained to set the light.

My thoughts ricochet around my head, but just being with Ted, steady and methodical at his work, smooths them out. We're secure even in silence. If it weren't for the war, Ted would've retired from the service, and we'd live in a bungalow within sight and sound of his other love, the sea. I think he needs her salt kisses, and to hear her changing voice murmuring, even when he's in my arms.

'You be my ears,' he says now. I don't think he can hear the sea's whisperings anymore. Tonight, I point out the buzzing of planes criss-crossing the channel before they're visible, then he observes them with binoculars, records them in his log, like he's identifying a rare bird, not a fire-spewing machine bringing tragedy to innocent folk. I try not to think about the cities getting bombed. Every death is someone's son or daughter.

My mind circles back to earlier today. Standing in line at the butcher's, the Station's ration books pressed to my chest.

'Saw your Relief Keeper in The Cross Keys last night,'

says the butcher, a slick of blood coating his meaty hands. 'Nice that he and the Missus can get out now and again.'

I force a smile and concentrate on his hands. Bob, our Relief Keeper is single. Nancy, wife of George the Assistant Keeper, went to the village yesterday evening, dolled up to the nines, when George was on evening shift.

When I asked George about Nancy's trip out, he told me to mind my own business. I'm supposed to keep life on the station friendly and harmonious.

Ted grunts, bringing me back to now. 'Penny for 'em?'

I shake away the memory of George's anger. 'Nothing to report,' I say. It'll save till he's off duty.

I gaze at gathering clouds, obscuring the moon. Some people might find it lonely out here: just us, the sea and sky, and a few hundred crying seabirds. We get all varieties: the full range of gulls, cormorants, terns, albatross. A bird-watchers paradise, if it weren't for the twists of barbed wire tumbling down the rocks, snagging like brambles. Beyond are the wrecking waves, waves which don't care which side you're on, they'd just suck you under and smash you on the rocks if they could reach you. You don't mess with the sea, it's too powerful. Some days it can help, some days it hinders. Never trust it, Ted says.

We both hear the shouts and screams coming from the middle of the yard below us.

'Stay there,' orders Ted, and sprints down the spiral staircase like a younger man.

I lean against the window to see better. Nancy is screaming at George and Bob, telling them to leave each other alone.

They jump apart as Ted gives them what-for in his foghorn voice; he sends Nancy back to her cottage, reminds his keepers that proper Trinity House Men don't fight like commoners.

Then I hear planes. Not ours, wrong sound, and not on their usual path. The men don't look up, even though I wave frantically at them from the tower to get under cover. I launch myself down the curving staircase, all six flights, my footsteps out of time with my heartbeats. I'll get over to the cottages quick as I can. In a minute it'll be over, we'll laugh together. Bob and George will shake hands, Nancy'll say she means no harm.

Descending, I slide my hand along the brass rail, polished to a slippery smoothness. There's a massive thunderclap, then a tremor shakes the tower and I sit down on a stair, arms over my head.

When all is still again, in the muffled quiet, I step through the tower door which is hanging open, out into the compound.

A gritty mist hangs in the yard. Silence. Yawning before me is a crater, shrouded in dust. Nancy stands at the far side, hushed for once, though her mouth's working nineteen to the dozen, and I see the curve of her belly.

I turn and stumble back up the staircase. The emergency light! I don't hear the switches click as the cogs whirr back into life, but I get the pilot light lit with just a few seconds to go before our five minute light-up. The lenses splinter the light into myriad reflections and the beam sweeps across the dark sea. Mission successful.

In the service room, I pick up Ted's pen, and start to record a log entry below his immaculate handwriting. *Emergency light lit after compound bombed. Direct hit. Lives lost...* but my hand shakes too much to write anymore and the pen clatters to the floor. Now I can't see beyond the desolate rocks and obliterating waves, and I capsize.

Yet Another 'Missing Children' Poster Adorns the Lampposts of a North-East Fishing Village

Kathy Hoyle

SNOW PELTS LAURA as she walks, ice-sharp and bruising. Gulls shriek, dusk falls, shadows prowl. She passes the fishmongers as the shutters come down, side-stepping Mr Dawson in his white overall, smeared with cod guts. She keeps her head bowed; she has no time for pleasantries. Fear is anchored, cold in her belly.

Laura is hardy. *Tough as old boots, that bairn,* nanna used to say, *it's her Viking blood.*

Laura isn't tough because of any bloodline. She'd learnt to toughen up on her eighth birthday when Mam had thrown a party. Her own friends hadn't been invited, only swaying adults in gaudy colours, smoking weed and dancing to 'the oldies'. Mam's laugh was high, like tinkling glass, her disapproval merciless. She'd grabbed Laura's chin and made her take a slug of vodka. *Lighten up, pet.* Later, when the music stopped and the house empty, Mam had kicked Laura's thin ribs with the point of her mauve shoe. Laura had marvelled when the bruises turned the exact same colour as the shoe.

Laura has learnt to feel nothing. Snow slices her cheeks. She doesn't pull up her collar against the wind. Her only thought is Eddie.

'Howay, please, Laura, the forecast isn't *that* bad,' Eddie had whined that morning.

When he was small, Mam had licked her thumb and smoothed his fringe, made him patty fishcakes at teatime and called him Blue, on account of his Viking eyes. Of course, she soon got bored. Even Eddie's baby blues couldn't hold her forever. Now, it was Laura he whined at, whose bed he wet, the warm spread of piss waking them both every morning at four, regular as clockwork.

'Eddie. You cannet take a boat out in January. Divn't be so daft.'

'It's been months. You said the new year.' He'd pulled at her cardigan.

'I meant April, Eddie, not friggin' January. Snow's comin'.'

'Da would have let us.'

Laura had rubbed toast crumbs from his jutted chin and zipped up his coat.

'I've telt ya. You gan near that boat and Peg'll come.'

Eddie had sucked in a breath; his love of the boat was always tempered by his terror of Peg Powler.

'That's just a daft story,' Eddie had countered, but his eyes were wary. Their Da had often warned them about Peg Powler, telling the tale on dark nights as the coal crackled in the fire. How the green-haired hag of the North Sea sits in wait for children who dare to come too close to the shore, then drags them into freezing water and feasts on their flesh.

Eddie had grabbed Laura's hand as she tried to leave. She'd prised his fingers away, shouted, 'You're to gan to Ryan's after school, Eddie! Not that boat, y'hear!'

She'd left him on the step, tears threatening.

Later, the head had walked into chemistry class pulling at his tie. Laura knew he'd come for her. It was always her.

'Laura, pet, come with me?'

Sniggers had rolled off her back as she followed him to his office. He'd pulled up a chair so close she could smell the coffee on his breath. She'd tugged down her skirt as he spoke.

'Eddie didn't turn up at his school this morning. They can't seem to geta hold of your mam... I can drive you home if you like? The weather's terrible.'

Laura had given him her best withering glare. *As if* life would be easier after a ride in the headteacher's car.

LAURA WALKS PAST her house, no point going in, that

would mean waking Mam, a stinging slap, or worse. The snow has eased, but the wind still chafes. She takes the path down through the sand dunes. The sky is ink-black but she's not afraid, she could find her way to the boat blindfold. The thin soles of her shoes slip but she keeps on, eventually emerging onto a wet strip of shingle. She scans the angry water.

Da's amble coble rocks furiously. Cobles are hardy, meant for the sea, but small boys are not. Laura imagines Eddie's thin arms desperately trying to hold the rudder, the biting North East wind lifting his shirt to bare a crown of blue-green bruises on his back. She pulls off her jacket, squints against the biting wind. She thinks of Eddie's tiny hand holding hers, in police stations, hospital waiting rooms, the back of a social worker's cars. She swallows down shame. She had wanted just one normal day, a movie with Michael Edwards, milkshake kisses, maybe a promise to call. But that had meant letting go of Eddie. She'd thought the novelty of tea at Ryan's house might be enough. The lure of a full belly…but for Eddie, the lure of Da's boat was stronger.

Laura takes off her coat, shudders, then slips off her shoes; shingle nips the soles of her feet. Over the roar of the water, she thinks she hears a faint cry. *Eddie!* She wades in. The cold takes her breath. It's sharp, sharp like the shock of a pointed shoe, the snap of a belt on raw skin, the bitterness of vodka.

Laura kicks hard, *I'm coming Eddie.* Memories flood her...scrubbing vomit from Mam's bedclothes, hiding in school toilets from classmate's sneers, holding her breath as the headteacher's hand creeps up her thigh, Da in a silk-lined box.

She lets the current carry her out towards Eddie, face down in the black water, bobbing ... like bait.

His fragile body pommels the coble's sturdy hull, his hand tethered by the mooring rope. The cleat clangs relentlessly. Laura's lungs are bursting. She grabs Eddie's pale hand, pulls it free from the rope. She clasps her fingers around his. *I won't let go.*

PEG POWLER MOVES swiftly, teeth bared, green tendrils flying. Her piercing shriek echoes across the breakers. Laura cries out for a mother who will never come. Her hand slips from Eddies, as the hag drags her down, down, into the black depths of the savage North Sea.

The coble rocks and the cleat clangs, relentlessly.

Button Bus
Chris Cottom

THE OLD LADY raising her arm at the Co-op bus stop has a jaunty feather in her hat, like William Tell.

'You don't need to wave, you know,' I say as she shuffles aboard. 'I always stop here.' The Felixstowe loop: eight times a day, five days a week, more if I want weekend overtime. Which, since Mandy left, I do.

It's mostly passes and contactless now, but this one's fumbling in her bag for so long she's endangering my timetable targets. I'll lose my bonus if I'm not parked up in bay seven within the four-minute window allowed by a management that doesn't believe in roadworks. She's got to be pushing eighty, probably from the wrong side.

'Do you want to sit down, love? You can show me your pass when you get off.'

Shit, she's proffering a coin.

Except it isn't a coin. It's a button.

In twenty-seven years I've been offered plenty of fags, a few swigs of Special Brew, the occasional spliff, and even a blowjob. But never a button.

'Where to, love?'

'Fairyland please.'

I click the cab camera off. There's an override switch I'm not supposed to know about.

'Single or return?'

'Could you decide for me?'

'Best make it a return.'

I take the big green button and check my mirrors. I wait for her to sit down but she doesn't move.

'Excuse me,' she says, holding out her hand. 'You haven't given me my change.'

SHE WAVES ME down again on Tuesday.

'Return to Toyland please young man.'

I laugh. 'No one's called me young for a long time. Sure you don't want Specsavers?'

She giggles like a schoolgirl and pays with two buttons, a flowery blue one and a red one with black spots like a ladybird.

I'm ready this time. I hand her one I'd snipped off a jacket I'd earmarked for the Age UK shop.

She waves it away. 'Keep the change.'

ON WEDNESDAY SHE'S carrying a battered chocolate box. The lid has a faded gold bow and a picture of a thatched cottage against an impossibly blue sky.

'My life savings,' she says. 'I'm off on my holidays.'

'Lovely jubbly. Where're you going?'

'Well,' she says, handing me the box. 'How far will this take me?'

'Scotland I should think. Easily.'

'Oh! I'd love to see Scotland.'

I lift the lid. The box is a coral reef of buttons: cerise hearts and serge-trouser greys, lilac toggles and imitation leathers, wooden-rimmed blues and flower-shaped pinks, filigreed silvers and Celtic knots.

'Best go and sit down, love.'

There's a guy in a cheap suit lurking at the stop by the Leisure Centre: a spot-check by Audit Central. I can clock those company clipboards from fifty yards. Some wet-behind-the-wipers graduate smartass desperate to assess my mirror management and count my smiles per mile.

The Button Lady is my only fare. I put my foot down.

'Scotland, love?' I call. 'Hold tight.'

The Weathering
Martha Lane

WE INVITED THE sea to dinner. A short sharp trill of the doorbell announced its arrival, cut short as the circuits fried under the force.

'No worry, we can fix that.' Our smiles painted on. Picasso awkward. 'Come in, come in. No need to take off your shoes.' Thin laughter. Scooby Doo nervous.

It filled our hallway, the sea, briny breath fetid with the rot of seaweed, sand-crusted teeth gnashing, frothing foaming saliva dripping onto the carpet. Slick green algae bloomed in its wake. Salt-crystal frost blossomed on every surface.

When it roared its hello, the deep boom clawed at our ears until they bled. Our wounds seared in its saline spittle. Hands politely kept away from our haemorrhaging ears; we beckoned the ocean further into the house. Unable to back out of the visit now. The sea wrecked the walls, smashed and shattered our knick-knacks and trinkets. All those things we thought were important. Each step swallowed the toys left out, weathered them into something unrecognisable, wore them down to nothing.

It sat, turned our sofa into splinters.

We offered plates of olives, cheese and crackers, poured wine by the bottleful. Anything to keep our hands busy, anything to distract from the shipwrecks and bodies, the shivers of sharks creeping past. Everything lost to the sea's distended stomach.

We warned them, of course, we warned the kids that the sea was coming to dinner. But stopping children being curious is as difficult as stopping the tide. As halting hurricanes, or restricting riptides. One of them, our middle – independent, impulsive, wild as the waves – touched its great side. The thunderous churn cut his fingers, the water as solid and sharp as shears.

A scalpel.

A scythe.

The ocean whipped around in a challenge. Didn't care that it was faced with a child. It swelled to a height completely unfathomable, coral reef veins throbbing, distorting. Curves and crests writhing. It wrenched the roof from the house, came back studded with stars. The child was nowhere to be seen.

We didn't mention it. Pretended not to notice while our eyes glistened. Pearls caught in the surf. Our strained mouths made Mona Lisa smiles. The empty chair between us almost as large as the sea itself.

'Have you enjoyed yourself?' We asked in unison, a practised parrot of something we might once have said before the sea came to visit. It nodded its colossal head in response, breakers beating down on the table, carving it in two.

It gathered its currents, heaved itself up, briefly surveyed the damage it had caused. Didn't care, caused more on its way to the door. It didn't say thank you. We waved it goodbye, the four of us. Waved to an uninterested back. It never turned round to look. Not once. We watched it shrink as it returned to its bed, lay flat, surface rolling as it digested the dinner we'd served.

A Cast of Crabs

Bernadette Stott

IT WAS JUST there, near those slippy stone steps that the kid fell off the seawall. And it was over there, near the bench that Jamie jumped in after him, half-drunk and half-brave. We'd all been fishing for crabs. The mum and dad, her pretty and him handsome, were a good twenty yards and ten years away from me and Jamie. The tide had been high when we started, long tall Jamie just able to touch his toes to the water.

Jamie had the day off, the week off, hell he probably had the whole summer off after another sacking. This pub landlord thought he was hiring a free bouncer. I wasn't there the night Jamie earned his sacking, but I bought the frozen peas for his left eye and it was me that taped up his broken finger. So we were spending the last of his earnings on a few bevvies in the harbour when we saw the little family of three fishing off the seawall and thought, 'fuck it, that looks a laugh'. We bought bacon and beer and then a bucket and two crab lines. You take off the hook, tie on the bacon and lower it from the seawall and wait. Meanwhile you kiss and swig beer and swing your legs, watching the water draining away like a giant's bath.

The surface was several meters below Jamie's trainers when we heard the pretty mummy ask, 'so what's a group of crabs called I wonder?' Local accent.

Handsome daddy sounded Home Counties as he rolled his eyes and replied, 'the collective noun', he was proud of knowing this, 'would be school or shoal, of course.' Pretty mummy opened her mouth to speak and then closed it again. Jamie looked at me and I looked at him.

Our bucket had four crabs and the sun was dipping with intent to the west, when there was a splash followed by a heartbeat, then a scream. Then Jamie dropped from the seawall like a bag of rocks. Hours that were actually minutes passed and then a grinning Jamie was dripping up the slippery steps. He was moving my way as I turned, smiling to the parents, half-dead with pride.

And then a hand flashed out. Husband-father hit wife-mother. Smack. Flat palm on pretty cheek, and time seemed to falter and stop. It restarted with Jamie throwing a sobbing wet bundle of boy into my arms and roaring with fury, fists bundling towards the once perfect family. And then Jamie was hitting and hitting and the noise of fist on flesh moved me back and away, while a small crowd moved forwards and towards.

And I heard Jamie roar, 'it's a CAST of crabs, you fuckwit!'

You know what I didn't realise though? What I only found out later? You don't get to keep the crabs. You have to put them all back in the sea, ready for some other bugger to catch them again. And again.

Deep Secrets
Brendan Praniewicz

HAS THIS EVER happened to you? You steal your neighbour's dog, and the two of you eat two whole packs of bologna together and listen to The Rolling Stones for an hour, and you tell the dog stories about all of your favourite past lovers, and the dog is into it, and for once in your life you've finally found someone who really listens!!! And when your neighbour realizes the dog is missing, and goes down the street in a fit of rage to look for it, you sneak the dog back inside his house like nothing happened. And when your neighbour comes back and asks, 'Bro, did you steal my dog, again?' And you offendedly reply, 'Do I look like someone who would steal your dog? I CAN BARELY TAKE CARE OF FREAKIN MYSELF, LET ALONE YOUR STUPID DOG, MAN.' And the whole week every time you see your neighbour, he keeps talking about how every time The Rolling Stones comes on the radio, his dog wags his tail and runs to the fridge like he's been classically conditioned and stuff, and your neighbour keeps going on and on and on about how his dog has diarrhoea, but you don't say anything, you just tune out and nod your head in silence, because you have diarrhoea too, and you don't want to be the only suspect in a dog heist.

Asking for a friend who has nothing to do with dogs.

Hands

Gillian Brown

DAWN SEEPS THROUGH the window as Dylan's broad hand pulls back the duvet on his side of the bed. For a second, in my half-sleep, I panic. But these are not the hands I have nightmares about. These are the hands that love me. My muscles relax. I breathe again.

Dylan creeps out to the kitchen. I feign sleep. Our ritual. A click. He's switching on the kettle for his tea. I visualise his fingers tensing around the handle of his mug as he flings in a teabag. Next, he places my cup under the espresso machine's nozzle with well-practised precision. Fresh coffee aromas invade my nostrils and tease my taste-buds. I hear the hiss as he froths the milk. Hand steady.

I sneak a look as he steps back into the bedroom. One hand delicately holds my coffee cup and the other grips his mug of tea. After lowering mine onto the bedside table, he taps my shoulder. A big man. A gentle touch. Love radiates from his fingertips. My skin tingles. My insides purr like a cat.

Dylan wields shovels and tips cement out of mixers all

day. His palms are calloused and hardened. The backs are bruised and a livid scar runs down his thumb. Yet his caress is as sensual as Ravel's Bolero.

He has mood swings like everyone else. When he's up, he is tender and gentle. His finger traces down my neck and between my breasts. Or he turns wild, sweeping me up in his arms and kissing me with inexhaustible passion. When he is down, he slaps things around. Objects. Never me. He tosses papers about, clenches his fists, or smacks the wall. I cower away. Hide.

The ghost of my ex-husband still lurks. His smooth, unlined hands fooled me at first. They wrote me poetry and love songs. After the wedding, those same hands became fists. The bruises have healed but shadows remain.

I open my eyes as Dylan starts to talk. It is his hands – more than his words – that express his thoughts. Pictures in the air tell me how much he loves me, how he'll miss me, how his day will be at work. He tips the last gulp of tea down his throat. His not-so-little pinkie curls up from the handle, as if he's at some fancy tea party, not about to be covered in brick-dust and dirt.

Before leaving, he strokes my hair, then lays a hand on my forearm. Reassuring. Affectionate.

Turning to look, I suddenly stiffen. The crinkly black hairs on the back of his hand turn to wire. His fingers to steel. I see both his hands now, gloved and taut, clamped around my ex's neck. I stifle a scream.

Sensing the tension, Dylan gives my arm a soothing rub. The image fades. I sink back into the pillows. Dylan slips out. The door whispers closed behind him.

Paper

Elle Symonds

EVERYONE AT SCHOOL is talking about what happened at the fairground.

'The incident', that's what the newspaper calls it. I spot the word on Dad's copy as he grips it in his hands. His face is concealed behind it, like it is every morning. On the front is a picture of the old lady who fell and died. She's smiling. Her face is all distorted by the paper's crease and the way it crinkles under Dad's fingers, as if her smile is one wide, grey line. Her inky eyes stare into mine.

'Terrible, isn't it?' says Dad.

I say yes. Everyone at school says it's terrible. Because the old lady died, the police have blocked part of the fairground with bright yellow tape. Peter Smith said they've put a huge padlock on the gates, which is where you buy tickets, and that it probably won't be open again for the rest of the summer.

When Dad says it's terrible I think that's what he means. That we can't go next weekend like we'd planned, and buy candy floss and get dizzy on rides. But maybe

Dad's talking about the old lady.

Dad shakes his head and has another sip of tea.

Mum sips hers. She holds the cup right up to her face and keeps it there, blowing on it softly, and takes tiny sips like a mouse.

'Such a shame,' Dad says, and closes the paper.

Dad isn't sad, because it won't be *us*. It won't ever be us. Dad watches the news and he shakes his head and then says something normal like, 'what's for dinner?' or 'we need more bread' or 'did you see the Williams' new car?'

Dad knows it won't be us. There's a bubble around our house. It's invisible. When danger comes it bounces off it. *Bounce bounce bounce.* In our house we're safe and fine and nothing can get us in our bubble.

Mum doesn't see the bubble, only the cracks. There are cracks in the bubble, she says, tiny, unseen fractures, and danger doesn't bounce, it creeps. It comes right up close and finds the gaps, forcing its way inside, so small you can barely notice. Like tiny, invisible snakes.

Mum worries about monsters. She says, *be careful.* She says they lurk everywhere, in all the places we can't see. They reach out from bushes and darkened streets with thin, spindly arms. They leap from white vans. They pull you inside, behind a door that roars shut, and take you far, far away. Anyone can be a monster, Mum says, you can't be too careful, no no. They sneak through windows at night. They come in different forms, like friends or neighbours or fairground workers who let you go on a ride even though it's not safe.

Dad gets up. Mum takes another slow sip of tea. She doesn't look at the lady's face on the paper. As if by looking at it, she's let the monsters in.

The Buttero

Christopher Santantasio

MY GRANDFATHER HEARD the snap of taut leather. From the corner of his eye, he saw the speckled mare pull loose from her harness, upending a fruit cart. Yellow apples thundered underfoot as the driver rushed to grab the bridle. My grandfather watched him stumble. The mare's right forehoof caught the driver on the side of the head, a quick jab that crumpled him into the fruited dirt. A young girl fainted against a nearby building just as a police officer pushed through the frantic crowd, weapon drawn.

It was New York City, 1910. My grandfather, still a young man, carried a tall crook as a walking stick. Back in Maremma, the men of his family had used it to unlatch pasture gates while herding bison on horseback. As the mare reared and the people scattered, my grandfather raised his crook and knocked the gun from the officer's hand. Two other officers quickly emerged from the crowd and wrestled him to the ground. They shouted in a language he couldn't understand. They snapped his crook in two. They beat him with clubs while the first officer retrieved his gun. The whole block shook when the mare hit the ground. It was my grandfather's second week in America.

He knew how to handle a startled horse, but he didn't have the language to tell them. My grandfather came from a family of butteri, mounted herders from the Italian lowlands. His ancestral home was near the Tyrrhenian coast where pasture rippled like a bedspread, an abundance of soft linen freckled with rosemary and heather, stretched over the hills. His father had defeated Buffalo Bill in a bronco riding contest twenty years earlier, when the famous American brought his Wild West Show to Italy. Bruised and alone in a jail cell, my grandfather wanted only to tell his captors how Buffalo Bill left Italy in shame without paying the wager he'd lost in that contest of spirit and skill.

After he was released, my grandfather found work at a tailor shop. Eventually, he saved enough to buy the business, laying the foundation of a comfortable life for himself and his family. Meanwhile, back in his homeland, the butteri were in decline. By the time I was born, there was only a handful left. They saw their land taken bit by bit—their livelihoods supplanted by machines—while my grandfather bounced three generations on his knee, telling stories in his adopted tongue.

My son's favourite is the one about the speckled mare

rampaging through the market: New York City, 1910. My grandfather tells him of a fearless buttero who swings onto the horse's back, guides her down an empty alley, and feeds her an apple from the gutter. One hand tight on his crook, the buttero speaks gently to the horse in his own tongue. He runs his fingers through her brindled mane. He tells her that this country will never tame him.

The Five Stages of Grief
Anita Goodfellow

Denial

IT IS RARE for passengers on a cruise ship to fall overboard.

She was at work when her stepfather called with the news, his voice distant. At first she thought it was one of his sick jokes.

No body had been recovered so they held a memorial service instead of a funeral. The photo he'd chosen showed them on board the cruise ship, dressed in their finery, sipping cocktails. She would feel different if Mum were dead, but she felt the same.

Her mother would come home.

Anger

MOST PEOPLE WHO fall off cruise ships either do so intentionally or by behaving recklessly.

The only careless thing Mum had ever done was to remarry. She didn't go to their wedding and couldn't forgive her mother for forgetting Dad so soon after his death. Where the hell was her step-father when Mum disappeared? She insisted on seeing the cruise company's records and became an expert on figures, tides and safety. She bombarded them with questions. The last sighting of her mother was in the cocktail bar.

Her mother always liked to let her hair down.

Bargaining

IF SOMEONE FALLS overboard the ship will turn around to search for the person. The success rate for finding people alive stands at 25%.

When Mum came back, she would be kinder to her stepfather. After all, he'd loved her mother or so he said. He also said he'd never set foot on a *bloody* boat again. She tried not to mind when he started clearing out Mum's stuff and instead offered to take everything to a charity shop. Of course she kept it all. She flicked through old photograph albums. There was an adolescent Mum holding a trophy – the county junior champion for breaststroke.

Her mother was a strong swimmer.

Depression

TIDES AND OTHER factors may mean that a passenger is far from their original location when the ship returns.

For days she didn't bother getting up. Calls remained unanswered. The compromise she reached with her step-father was not to see him. She couldn't rid herself of the image of Mum on an exotic island sunning herself on a sandy beach in that ridiculous magenta bikini.

Her mother was out there waiting to be found.

Acceptance

THERE HAVE BEEN no incidents of passengers falling off cruise ships due to the negligence of cruise companies.

Now, when she catches her face in the mirror she sees traces of her mum in the lines around her mouth. When she got a call from the hospital she tried to feel something. Anything. He'd listed her as his next of kin. He wanted his ashes to be scattered in the local park.

The sea is steel grey and the sky heavy with the threat of rain. She unscrews the lid of the urn and tips out the contents. The wind catches the fragments before the water claims him. He always hated the sea.

Her mother isn't coming back.

The Turning Point
Richard Hooton

TODAY'S THE BIG day. Your grin is almost rictus.

Perhaps there should be cards, songs, flowers?

The old boiler's not yet kicked in to fight off winter. You huddle within your stiff blazer. Mr Unwin's droning about black holes and seeing stars that burnt out long ago. You prefer physics – much more measurable – to chemistry's mysteries and biology's awkwardness.

Mark pokes your ribs, displays Insta on his cracked screen. Your selfie filtered to fuck.

'You're so fugly.' His fingers lash as he trolls.

'QUIET!' The besuited, bespectacled teacher glowers. You shrink under the heat of their stares like fresh meat in a frying pan.

Different school, same problems. Always a relish to scuff the shine off the new kid, to hold them down. Children can be so cruel, they said. But you know that's not restricted to youngsters.

HIM, GLARING AS if you're pathetic: 'Stand up for yoursen. Fight back.'

Her, gazing as if you're pitiful: 'Walk away. Don't engage.'

(Different houses, different rules, different opinions.)

You: A shuttlecock batted between.

THE BELL TOLLS for lunch. Bags grabbed, chairs scraping, a gush for the exit.

Maybe mark the occasion with a photograph, a sketch, a painting?

You follow behind, no appetite anymore. It's eaten you from the inside. Turns out the previous time wasn't a cry for help but a practice run.

Mr Unwin stops you. You focus on his bristly moustache, mirror his rigid smile.

'You look happier,' he says. 'Good to see.'

Silence.

He leaves you be.

Heading for the toilet cubicle; your safe space. Crowded corridors. Rushing. Laughing. Pushing. Bickering. Lynx masks sweat.

Shadow walk, out the way, unnoticed.

A letter, poem, note?

Unlike Mr Unwin, you can't explain black holes and failing stars. You've no whiteboard on which to spell it out then wipe clean away.

Nearly there.

You enter. Quiet. Alone.

You close the door for the last time. Rest on the toilet seat. Take from your rucksack the jar of paracetamol, the bottle of water. Undo the caps.

Deep breath. Empty your mind. Just swallow.

A respectful knocking startles you.

The door swings open.

Mr Unwin crouches. Looks at you with eyes containing things that can't be written on a whiteboard.

'You won't always feel like this,' he says softly. 'Things get better. Trust me.'

He takes the pills from your trembling hand.

And shepherds you to safety.

What My Therapist Calls Grounding To Calm My Triggered Body

Rosaleen Lynch

FIVE THINGS I see—a stray dog, a retreating canal boat opening up the green algae like splitting a pea pod, maybe that's three, a moorhen building a nest, a used condom in the weeds and my wavering reflection in the water where I've thrown my journal.

Four things I hear—the stray dog's bark at the moorhen and her flutter of wings, the put-put engine of the canal boat, the judder of the cars on the bridge over a speed bump, your shoes echo under the bridge fading, the splash of my journal but not of my cigarette, diving into the ripple, lit end in and submerging, but popping out at the filter and now, flat unmoving in the water, even when the edge of the canal bank crumbles in, stones dropping, earth floating.

Three things I feel—the stray dog nuzzling my leg, and I let him, the vibration of the cars overhead, the panic, no you meant thing I feel physically, no I feel panic, I feel my heartbeat, no I feel both, do I have two heart beats?

Two things I smell—everything stinks, the stray dog stinks, the canal stinks, everything stinks.

One thing I taste—the extra strong mint I'm sucking so Mum doesn't know I've been smoking to cover up the taste and the smell of you.

Scratch Art For Grown Ups
Sally Curtis

MY TEACHER SHOWED me, when I was five or six, how to cover an entire piece of card in wax crayon: a mad rainbow of deranged lines, colours clashing, dashing across the page, like the scribble of screams, a scrawl of confusion.

After, I brushed thick black paint, night-time dark, over the frenzy, camouflaging the chaos until all my colours were hidden.

I had to wait a long time for it to dry but I learned patience.

Then I learned strength.

And then precarious trust.

Now, as you softly scrape at the hardened layer, scratch by scratch glimpses of another life fumble through the darkness into the light.

America

Sherri Turner

'AMERICA,' SHE SAID. 'I'm going to America.'

'Really?' one of her colleagues said. 'America? Are you sure?'

As though someone could easily be mistaken about such a thing, a person like her in any case.

The mutterings continued as she gathered the few personal belongings from her desk into a carrier bag, but she zoned them out. America had been a great idea. Make a plan and stick to it, her father used to say. So she had and she would.

On the bus on the way home she clutched the bag to her still flat stomach and held her pride close to her for warmth.

When the baby was born she named him George, after Washington, and she bounced him on her knee, ignoring the rising damp in the council flat, and told him stories of how she would take him to America one day.

Body of Christ
Moira McGrath

BREDA SHUFFLES TOWARDS the altar. Head held back, open-mouthed with eyes closed, she accepts the wafer-thin Eucharist in the old-fashioned way she learnt as a child.

Sixty years earlier, a young girl kneels in the confessional box; air heavy with sweat and oppression. Silently, the priest slides in behind her, his fleshiness disguised by his incense infused soutane.

Holding her head back, he squashes her open-mouthed, distorted face against the grille, in the old-fashioned way.

'Amen.' Breda turns from young curate dragging her secrets back to her pew. With her gnarled hands clasped around her rosary, she prays for forgiveness.

Cornfields
Diane D. Gillette

I RAN FERAL through cornfields that summer. Forging a trail through stalks double my height until reaching a clearing and making it my secret fairy bowl. I'd tumble down, drowning under the sticky humidity that coated every inch of me, aching for the mountain air that sustained me. I wished to be airlifted back home, but there were no corn fairies, and if I strained hard enough, I could still hear my parents fighting from 500 miles away. The cornfield always released me molasses-drip slow. I'd crawl up the back steps of the farmhouse sometime before supper, letting the screen door slam behind me. Grandma waited with a damp cloth to wipe the dust from my face. Quick fingers checked my cornsilk hair for ticks before she kissed the top of my head and gave me a glittering look that said she once ran through cornfields too.

I Am Sailing, Very Far Away
S.A. Greene

Dawn

GRINNING PORPOISES ARC out of the water into the repressed sparkle of the morning haze. I wish I could film them for my great-nephew – this was all his idea – but we surrendered our smartphones before boarding.

Luncheon

THE CLINK OF silverware on china earths me to less uncertain times. Phoebe says she's never seen personalised napkin rings before. She's young. Too young.

Reflections from the chandeliers blink orange in the bowl of my spoon like fracturing suns.

Nights

THREE WEEKS OUT and the food's still decent, but I notice things: tinned vegetables appear; fellow-passengers fade.

Phoebe's gone. Nobody mentions it.

A million stars cup our tiny ship but not one will tell me where we're going, so in my darkening cabin I imagine sitting next to Captain Salvatore, the brush of his white sleeve electrifying every hair on my forearm as he works his silver-plated fish-knife into the salmon.

It's A Beautiful Day For A Picnic, But You're Not Invited

Laurie Marshall

SWEAT SOAKS MY blouse as I hike to our favourite mountain top. Your insulated pack is stuffed with the most offending bits: truffle eyes scooped out on a shell-shaped sugar spoon, spaghetti strings snipped with pasta shears. Your tuna steak tongue released easily – no surprise – with the sushi knife you offered as an apology for my second ER visit. Your sausage fingers were separated from your fleshy palm by granddad's butcher knife. It dismantled many a feral creature in his hand. In mine, it smashed your skin and marrow into the walnut cutting board you used to break my jaw.

No Rain

Di Spence

ON MOVING DAY, she didn't pack more than her agreed share of the CDs. She didn't toss her wedding band down a storm drain as she waddled into town in search of coffee. She didn't kick over the neatly arranged al fresco chairs and tables, nor imagine him en route to St Pancras to see the girl he'd met three weeks ago whom he now "couldn't live without". Instead, she sat and sipped her decaf. And feeling the warmth of her hand on the bump, she wondered why the sun had to be so cruel as to shine that day.

Robert

Kevin Sandefur

WHEN I WOKE up yesterday, we were all named Bob. I noticed it while going to work. I looked around and thought: *we're all Bobs on this bus.* It wasn't so bad one on one, but in meetings, whenever I'd say 'Hey, Bob,' everyone would have to look at me to see who I meant.

Last night I went home with someone from the club and in the heat of our passion they called out 'Oh, Bob' and I wondered which of us they were thinking of. On the other hand, this time I remembered their name. It was Bob.

Today when I got up everyone had my face, or maybe I had theirs. At least today we have faces. It's confusing, so tonight I took a purple Sharpie and put the tiniest of dots behind my left eyebrow, where no one can see, but I will know it's there.

Tom's Toy Gun
Connie Boland

ON THE DAY before her sixth birthday, Tom promised to give his sister a piece of double bubble, comic strip included, if she would help him set up a lemonade stand. He coaxed Pearl into a frilly white dress but said she could leave off the black shoes.

Tom said Pearl looked just like Shirley Temple, her favourite TV star.

Liquid splashing into a tall glass, its backward leap toward the rim, sends Tom spiraling to that long ago summer day. Beads of condensation sparkling on the pitcher conjure images of a busy street. He remembers a cloud grey Buick gliding to the curb.

'I'll have a drink,' the stranger said.

Tom told their parents he slept soundly that night; a new toy cap gun cradled in his arms. The chewed gum, with tiny teeth marks, hardened on Pearl's bedpost. She was never found.

You Said You'd Always Wait For Me
Kate Simblet

WE STAGGERED, SWAGGERED, through teenage years. Poleaxed on ciders in precinct doorways. My chin on your shoulder, we drank in the stillness, haunting the darkness.

The locals, so vicious, swooped on your mother; that unflinching town more brutal than its architecture. She'd scavenged like a seagull to put food on the table—working the backstreets, she was easy to label. But when I look back, to when you were accused, did rumours cut deeper than glass?

You promised, someday, we'd see the ocean, but I'd clung to you knowing if I didn't leave soon, time would run away like the rats down the subways—and like concrete, you'd always stay there. So one night after we fumbled goodbyes, I left you to seek salty air.

After they accused you, you vanished—no trace. Did the mob find their quarry, or did you escape? Leaving our ghosts trapped in the shadows.

The Authors

Susan Iona Swan

Susan Iona Swan's short fiction has been short listed in various competitions including the 2021 Costa Prize, the Alpine Fellowship 2021 Award and the 2021 Trip Fiction Prize, but this is the first one she has won. Her stories have been published on Globe Soup and in anthologies. Last year, she self-published a novel, Last Chance Mill, about a couple of townies who relocate to an old mill in a Devon village to run art holidays. What could possibly go wrong? She lives by the sea in Devon.

Emma Naismith

Emma is a Scot living in Sweden. She writes stories from a red house by the edge of a forest north of Stockholm.

Catherine Ogston

Catherine Ogston writes flash fiction, short stories and longer fiction. Work has been published in National Flash Fiction Day anthologies, Bath Flash, Reflex Press, New Writing Scotland and others. She was the 2022 winner of the TL;DR Press flash contest. Her adult novel was highly commended at the Exeter Novel Prize while her YA novel has been longlisted at the Caledonia Award and Mslexia. She was shortlisted for a 2021 New Writers Award at the Scottish Book Trust and is currently shortlisted for the Kelpies Prize for Writing.

James Mason

James Mason has, in small and superficial ways, been a poet, editor and comedian. His work has been published in The Phare, Flash Fiction Magazine and Horla magazine, as well an anthology by Black Pear Press. He won the Tortive Theatre 101 Flash competition twice and had stories shortlisted in the 2020 Cranked Anvil and 2021 Worcester Lit Fest writing competitions. He lives in Worcester, UK.

Jess Moody

Jess Moody (she/her) is a writer and reviewer based in London, UK. Find her fiction in *Ellipsis Zine, The Interpreter's House, Lunate, Lucy Writers, JMWW, Janus, Northern Gravy,* and other fine places. Nominated for the *Pushcart Prize, Best of the Net*, and listed in the *BIFFY50*, her work has also been shortlisted in several competitions. Non-fiction features and reviews lurk in *Lunate, Bright Wall/Dark Room, ScreenSpeck* and *A Personal Anthology*. 'Grit' is the first story she wrote when she dared to give creating writing a whirl back in late 2019.
www.jmoodywriter.com @jesskamoody

Juana Riepenhausen

Juana Riepenhausen is an Argentinian writer based in London. She is passionate about exploring different genres and forms and considers writing her way of making sense of the human experience. She likes to drop her characters into uncertain situations and observe the choices they make to find answers. When she isn't working on her first novel, she champions artists through different workshops that focus on enjoying the creative process.

Iqbal Hussain

Iqbal has two short stories in upcoming anthologies – 'All Her Tomorrows', for *City of Stories Home* run by Spread the Word, and 'The Long Journey Home', for *Lancashire Stories* by Lancashire Libraries.

Iqbal is an alumnus of the HarperCollins Author Academy. He is one of fifteen emerging writers to feature in Inkandescent's *Mainstream*anthology, with 'The Reluctant Bride', a ghost story set in rural Pakistan. His short story 'A Home from Home' won gold prize in the Creative Future Writers' Awards.

Iqbal's semi-autobiographical novel, *Northern Boy*, about being a 'butterfly among the bricks', is currently out on submission.

Twitter: @ihussainwriter
Website: www.ihussainwriter.com

Paul J. Jackson

Paul J Jackson has recently been published in the Oxford Flash Fiction Anthology 'Sticks and Stones' with his story 'The Lover'. He has written three books, 'Secrets and

Lies', 'My Soul to Take' and an anthology of short stories titled, 'Down a Dark Path – sinister tales of supernatural horror'. All are on amazon now. He also has his own website www.pauljjackson.co.uk with links to his books.

Helen Chambers

Helen won the Fish Short Story in 2018 and was nominated for Best Microfictions in 2019 and a Pushcart Prize in 2021. She acts and directs in her local 'outdoor Shakespeare' group (but never at the same time!) and writes flash fiction and short stories. You can read some of her publications at:

helenchamberswriter.wordpress.com/writing

Kathy Hoyle

Kathy Hoyle's work can be found in publications such as Spelk, Virtualzine, Lunate, Ellipsiszine, Reflex Fiction, The Forge and The South Florida Poetry Journal. She has previously won the Retreat West Themed Flash Competition, came second in The Edinburgh Flash Fiction Award, and third in the Cambridge Flash Fiction Prize. and the HISSAC Prize. Other stories have been listed in competitions including, The Bath Flash Fiction Award, The Exeter Short Story Prize, the Fish Publishing Flash Fiction Prize, Flash 500, and Strands International. She holds a BA (hons) and an MA in Creative Writing and lives in a sleepy Warwickshire village in the UK with her crazy labradoodle.

Chris Cottom

Chris Cottom was the People's Choice Winner of the 2022 LoveReading Very Short Story Award, has won competitions with Shooter Flash and On The Premises, and placed third in competitions with Anansi Archive and Cranked Anvil. He was highly commended in the 2022 Bournemouth Short Story Writing Prize, shortlisted twice in the 2022 Parracombe Prize Short Story Competition, and has been long or shortlisted in thirty or so further competitions. He's had previous stories published by Retreat West as well as in Streetcake and broadcast on BBC Radio Leeds.

Martha Lane

Martha Lane is a writer by the sea. She predominately writes about nature and grief. Her stories (all of which can be found at marthalane.co.uk) have been published by Northern Gravy, Perhappened Mag, Bandit Fiction, Ellipsis Zine and Reflex Press among others. She's been nominated for a BIFFY50 and Best Microfictions and is a twice-winner of the Free Flash Fiction Competition. When she isn't writing she's reading, wrangling children, or paddling. Tweets @poor_and_clean

Bernadette Stott

Bernadette Stott is an emerging writer who is Canadian

by birth and British by situation. She lives with her husband and three children in London. The four of them like to gang up on her and make fun of her accent. She recently completed an English degree (with Creative Writing) at the Open University. She has had podium finishes in several short fiction competitions, including this one (!) and first place in the Cranked Anvil Flash fiction competition, in addition to long and short listings in several other UK short fiction prizes. She loves a quiz.

Brendan Praniewicz

Brendan Praniewicz earned his MFA in creative writing from San Diego State in 2007 and has subsequently taught creative writing at San Diego colleges. He has had short stories and poems published in Races Y Mas, the Watershed Review, Driftwood Press, Tiny Seed Literary Journal, and Gold Man Review. In addition, he received second place in a first-chapters competition in the Seven Hills Review Chapter Competition in 2019. He won first place in The Rilla Askew Short Fiction Contest last year.

Gillian Brown

Gillian Brown started out as a travel writer but her heart now lies in fiction. Her short stories have won and been shortlisted in various competitions – many published online.

She has won the Yeovil Literary Prize and had winning stories published in Writing Magazine and Writers' Forum. Her work has appeared in several anthologies. Amongst them, Bridge House, Hawkeye Books, Earlyworks Press, Writers Abroad and Stringybark.

Her story ideas are often triggered by her other passion – travelling.

Elle Symonds

Elle is a novelist and flash fiction writer from Bristol, UK. Her words have appeared at *101 Words, The Drabble, 5 Minute Lit, Crow & Cross Keys* and more. She's fond of the seaside, ghost stories and filling her house with too many books. You can find her on Twitter: @seventhelle.

Christopher Santantasio

Christopher Santantasio lives in Columbus, Ohio. His work has most recently appeared in Epiphany, One Story, Storm Cellar, and Smokelong Quarterly. New work is forthcoming in DIAGRAM. He was a finalist for the 2020 Chautauqua Janus Prize and the 2021 Iowa Review Fiction Award. He is at work on a novel and a collection of short stories.

Anita Goodfellow

Anita Goodfellow has an MA in creative writing from Bath Spa University. She divides her time between the UK and France. Her stories have been placed and shortlisted in writing competitions and published in numerous anthologies. In between novel writing she loves experimenting with flash. @nitagoodfellow

Richard Hooton

Born and brought up in Mansfield, Nottinghamshire, Richard Hooton studied English Literature at the University of Wolverhampton before becoming a journalist and communications officer. He has had numerous short stories published and has been listed in various competitions, including winning contests run by Segora, Artificium Magazine, Henshaw Press, Evesham Festival of Words, Cranked Anvil, the Charroux Prize for Short Fiction, the Federation of Writers (Scotland) Vernal Equinox Competition and the Hammond House International Literary Prize. Richard lives in Mossley, near Manchester, and is a member of Mossley Writers.

Rosaleen Lynch

Rosaleen Lynch, an Irish community worker and writer in the East End of London with words in lots of lovely places and can be found on Twitter @quotes_52 and 52Quotes.blogspot.com.

Sally Curtis

Sally Curtis lives in Bournemouth and started writing seriously about five years ago. Before becoming a primary school teacher, she had a varied career meeting plenty of interesting people and is also a qualified hypnotherapist. She has been published in Writers' Magazine and by Reflex Fiction and has been long and short-listed in several competitions (Flash 500, Susie Busby, Michael Terrance amongst them) so creeping ever onwards towards the winner's podium.

Sherri Turner

Sherri Turner has had numerous short stories published in magazines and has won prizes for both poetry and short stories in competitions including the Bristol Prize, the Wells Literary Festival and the Bridport Prize. Her work has also appeared in many anthologies and in various places online. She tweets at @STurner4077.

Moira McGrath

Having taught Drama for many years, Moira has written scripts, training materials and resources for teachers. Since retiring, she has enjoyed writing short stories, poems and travel blogs and was the winner of the 2017 H.E. Bates' national short story competition.

Diane D. Gillette

Diane D. Gillette (she/her) lives in Chicago. Her work is a Best Small Fictions selection. Her chapbook "We're All Just Trying to Make It to January 2nd" is available through Fahmidan & Co. Publishing. She is a founding member of the Chicago Literary Writers. Read more at www.digillette.com.

S.A. Greene

S.A. Greene writes short fiction in Derbyshire. She's had stories in Janus Lit., Sledgehammer, Ellipsis Zine, Funny Pearls, Free Flash Fiction, Reflex Fiction, Retreat West, and the 2022 Flash Flood anthology. She has recently noticed that most of her stories feature kitchens and/or tables and/or food.

Laurie Marshall

Laurie Marshall is a writer and artist living in Northwest Arkansas. She reads for Fractured Lit and her work has been published in Fictive Dream, Bending Genres, Versification, Janus Literary, and Flash Frog, among others. She placed 2nd in Retreat West's February 2021 Monthly Micro Competition and her longlisted story will appear in the 2021 Bath Flash Fiction Award anthology. Connect on Twitter @LaurieMMarshall.

Di Spence

After 15 years as a librarian, Di thought it was about time she stopped admiring the outside covers of other people's tales and started exploring the insides of some of her own. She has been published on the *Paragraph Planet* website and this is the first piece she has had shortlisted for a competition. She lives with her son, a fiery kitten and a peppy pup, and dreams of becoming a portrait artist.

Kevin Sandefur

Kevin Sandefur is the Capital Projects Accountant for the Champaign Unit 4 School District. His fiction has appeared (or is forthcoming) in *The Saturday Evening Post*, *The Gateway Review*, *The Sunlight Press*, *Pulp Literature*, and both the 2020 and 2022 Bath Flash Fiction anthologies. He lives with his wife and two cats in Champaign County, Illinois, which is a magical place where miracles happen almost every day, and hardly anyone seems to find that remarkable.

Connie Boland

Connie Boland is an award-winning freelance journalist and creative writer in Corner Brook, Newfoundland and Labrador.

Kate Simblet

Kate Simblet (she/her), social works by day, plays with words by night. Very happy she stumbled into flash fiction. Learning as she goes, and sometimes her words land lucky. Lives in Brighton, loves the sea. @KateSimblet

Lightning Source UK Ltd.
Milton Keynes UK
UKHW021258210822
407537UK00006B/124